Mack Bolan meets the beasts that bring fear to the night

In the first room on the ground floor was a torture chamber, containing whips, ropes, chairs nailed to the floor, motorcycle chains, brass knuckles. Bolan took two steps into the room, and the floor gave way beneath him.

Lunging desperately to one side, he leaped to safety. The trapdoor swung down, revealing a pit below. The bottom was filled with sharp punji sticks pointing upward, Nam style.

The Executioner moved away from that room to another door. He pushed it open.

In the dim light he saw six wooden cages, each holding a naked girl. All the girls were asleep except one. She looked at him in terror.

"Don't hit me again!" she cried. "I'll do it. I'll do anything now...."

MACK BOLAN

The Executioner

DON PENDLETON's EXECUTIONER

MACK BOLAN

Council of Kings

A GOLD EAGLE BOOK FROM

TORONTO · NEW YORK · LONDON · PARIS
AMSTERDAM · STOCKHOLM · HAMBURG
ATHENS · MILAN · TOKYO · SYDNEY

First edition July 1985

ISBN 0-373-61079-3

Special thanks and acknowledgment to Chet Cunningham
and Les Danforth for their contributions to this work.

Printed in Canada

"It does life good to have the devil in it, so long as you keep your foot planted firmly on his neck."
—*quoted to Bolan by Buddy, victim of the Council of Kings*

Dedicated to the dead of the Mekong.

1

Mack Bolan tensed as he sighted through the .460 Magnum Weatherby Mark V rifle's scope, tracking a man leaving a small store on West Burnside Street in Portland, Oregon. The man had entered ten minutes earlier, five minutes before the 5:30 P.M. closing time. Relaxed, Bolan eased his fingers on the trigger guard.

A soft misty rain fell. From the roof of the four-story building where he lay, the Executioner watched the man emerge from the store. He waited for the two others he knew would follow.

When the three were outside and the heavy door had been shut and locked, the Executioner fired on the man farthest from the wall. The firing-pin of his bolt-action, long-range hunting rifle ignited the primer in the .460 round, setting off the powder charge that shot a five-hundred-grain bullet through the twenty-six-inch, chrome-lined barrel at 2,700 feet per second.

The weapon's roar shattered the soft evening. The bullet tore into the man in the brown suit above the heart and slammed him back into his companions.

The Executioner ejected the used cartridge and chambered up another live round.

Sighting again, he adjusted his aim, considered the five hundred yards to the next target, and stroked the trigger.

The bullet hit the sky-blue-suited man beneath the left eye and bored into his skull, splattering his head against the building.

Bolan worked the bolt and kept his eye to the scope. The mist was turning to rain. The last man scrambled behind a heavy masonry planter.

The Executioner had to shoot before the target vanished. The round thundered from the big-game rifle with more than 8,000 foot-pounds of energy and ripped into the belly of the crouching figure, spinning him around and spilling his bowels, killing him.

Bolan retrieved the two spent shell casings, left the third in the chamber and moved to a door that led to the ground floor and a rear exit.

He was a half-mile away when the first Portland police car whined up to the scene. The rain made it probable that no one had seen him. No windows looked directly onto the roof of the building, the tallest for two blocks each way.

As Bolan drove the rented Thunderbird toward the waterfront, he thought how much this seemed like the first time—the time back at the beginning of the universe when he executed five members of a loan company because they had provoked his father, already upset over his daughter's forced prostitution, into an insane rage in which he killed his daughter and wife, injured his son Johnny, then turned the gun on himself.

The shots today had come from the same kind of

heavy-hunting weapon, a .460 Magnum Weatherby Mark V, a beast at ten and a half pounds and deadly as hell from half a mile away.

The Executioner had been attracted to this northwest city by the loan racketing that, partly due to high unemployment in the logging and lumber industry, had become epidemic. Pacific Family was the first on Bolan's hit list. He had been in town two days, digging up sources, making lists, gathering all the intel he could find on the Gino Canzonari family.

Bolan returned to Burnside and passed the death scene. Four police cars blocked the far lane. Two cops directed traffic. The Executioner continued down Burnside to Front Avenue and turned north, traveling downstream along the Willamette River.

On Front Street near Seventeenth Avenue, across from the Port of Portland Terminal One, is a small bar that draws a lot of working stiffs, stevedores and truckers taking a break before heading home.

Bolan parked the Thunderbird and entered the bar. It smelled of stale beer, smoke and sweat. He signaled for a draft and looked around. There were numerous booths, a long stand-up bar, an electric shuffleboard, two video games.

For a long time Bolan studied a medium-sized man with a cloth cap, Hawaiian sport shirt and tan pants who was playing solitaire in the far booth. This was Leo the Fish. The Executioner slid in across from him, his blue poplin jacket covering the silenced Beretta 93-R nestled in shoulder leather.

Leo was about to play another hand when Bolan

looked at him and cleared his throat. The man glanced up.

"Leo, hear you're the man around here to see for some quick money."

Leo squinted as smoke from his cigarette curled into his eyes. He moved it and dumped the ashes. The squinting, pale-blue eyes took in the Executioner unblinkingly for seconds before he answered, "Massachusetts, I'd say. I know accents. You from back there?"

"Close enough. How much can I get?"

"References. Who told you I dealt money?"

"My sister-in-law. She's married to this longshoreman. He said . . ."

Leo put up his hand. "How much you need?"

Bolan held open the jacket to shield his action from onlookers, then drew the Beretta so Leo could see it. Bolan lowered it under the table and pushed the muzzle into Leo's belly.

"I want all you have, Leo. Right now."

"Listen, I'm retired, this is just a little payday and a little fun. Keeping my hand in."

"Let's have the cash, Leo."

"I only got a thousand or so. Guys cleaned me out, lots of loans."

"I want the loan cards, too."

Slowly Leo reached in a shirt pocket and took out six 3x5-inch white cards. He laid them on the table facedown. His hand moved toward his hip pocket.

"Real easy, Leo. You're about a three-pound trigger pull from finding out if there's life after death."

"Hey, take it easy. I'm just getting the goods. I'm

not dumb.'' He eased a well-used leather billfold from his rear pocket and removed a sheaf of twenties and fifties.

The cash and cards vanished into a pocket of Bolan's jacket.

"Yeah, Leo the Fish, Chicago. You specialized in delivering a fish to the next of kin. That was your notice that the victim was now sleeping with the fish in Lake Michigan.''

"So sue me.''

"I will, exterminator. Move inside the booth. Against the wall.''

Leo's eyes searched the room for help, anything. A tinge of terror touched his closely shaven face.

"So long, scum. You just made your last transaction.''

The Beretta coughed twice in the noisy bar. The rounds were aimed upward under the table, and one of them tore into Leo's heart. Leo sighed, closed his eyes and dropped his head against the wall as if sleeping.

Bolan replaced the Beretta under his jacket and stepped from the booth. He tossed a black metal marksman's badge beside the dead man.

Outside he crossed a name off a list. Then he wheeled the Thunderbird across the Willamette River to the east side of Portland. He was acting exactly as he had in Vietnam. Identify. Infiltrate. Destroy. But the similarity, the necessity of war, grieved The Executioner.

THE GREATER BROTHERHOOD FINANCE COMPANY was well out on Southeast Powell, past Mount Tabor Park and toward Powellhurst, but still within city limits.

The one-story building stood between a hi-karate school and a small grocery. The building was dark. Bolan parked in the back alley, slung a small supplies pack over his shoulder and left the car.

He picked the lock on the back door of the finance company and stole into the place.

It was a highly efficient operation. Loan records were stored on a TRS-80 computer. Bolan found a file of 5 1/2-inch floppy diskettes marked Outstanding Loans and dumped them in a metal wastebasket.

On the wall was a computer printout graph that showed that interest payments had reached 186 percent of total payments on principal. In a legitimate loan operation the percentage would be fifteen or eighteen percent at most.

The Executioner closed the blinds on the front windows and tossed a white phosphorus grenade into each of the two main rooms.

The burning phosphorus splattered around both rooms the instant the grenades went off. It stuck to everything it hit and burned holes through anything flammable. The heat was intense and the flame impossible to extinguish.

The building was an older wooden one. The neighboring karate school was in a new concrete block structure that would not ignite easily. The safety of the building on the other side would depend on the Portland Fire Department.

As the flames took hold of the two rooms, Bolan went out the back door and drove away. So much for any outstanding loans.

He drove downtown and parked in the underground garage of the high-rise hotel he had checked into two days earlier. He covered the weapons, made sure the Thunderbird was gassed full and went up to his room.

He stared out his window at the masses of evergreens marching up the hills. The whole city was one green carpet, nothing like the brown semidesert of Southern California. Bolan realized how much he loved the Northwest.

But even here the cancer of the Mafia was destroying fine men and women. He felt a special empathy for its victims, something deep and personal and painful. He could never undo the tragedy of his family, but he could strike out to prevent other tragedies.

Because he despised them so, loan sharks would always be among his primary targets.

The Executioner planned to tear up the Canzonari family's loan division until its blood turned the Willamette River into a red flood.

2

Charlotte Albers heard the phone's tenth ring. Frustrated and frightened, she slammed down the receiver.

She wiped away tears and rubbed her eyes.

Dammit! This was the fifth time she had dialed her sister's number. Leen should have been home from work by now. Charlotte dialed again, making sure she hit the right numbers. The phone rang four times. Then someone picked it up.

Thank God!

"Leen! I've been calling for an hour. I've got to talk to you!" Charlotte spoke intently. "Look, I've got some trouble, big trouble." She fought back tears. "Leen, I need help!"

"Hey, take it easy. I'm here. We've always helped each other. Now tell me what this is all about."

Charlotte exhaled into the mouthpiece. "Leen, I need some money. Quite a bit."

"Is that it? How about a hundred and fifty...as a loan."

"That's not enough. I need twelve hundred and fifty by six o'clock tomorrow evening."

The line was silent. "Lot, you into coke again?"

"No, no. I just had some short money days, and I borrowed from a finance company...."

"A loan shark, right? Dammit, you know how those bastards operate." There was a pause. "Charlotte, I'm sorry. We just don't have that kind of cash laying around." She paused. "What happens if you can't pay?"

"I have a choice, get gang-banged or my arm broken."

"Charlotte!"

"Okay, it isn't that bad. But tomorrow night, the new interest is added. That's $250 more. I'm getting in deeper and deeper."

"They won't hurt you...."

"Younger sister, you don't know how they play."

"But if they hurt you, you'll never be able to pay them."

"They call it 'making an example.'"

"Who is it, Lot?"

"Jody Warren."

"That slime!"

"You want me to swish my ass into your bank and apply for a signature loan?"

"Baby, I'm sorry. If I'd known, we would have thought of something. Warren hurts people."

"Thanks for the support," Charlotte sobbed. "Look, I shouldn't have called. Jody said if I couldn't raise the cash, to come there tonight and we'd talk, work out something."

"You know what he's going to work out, baby. He's going to work you out of your panties."

"I'm no fragile little flower, Leen. So maybe I let

him play around a little. If I do, maybe I can put him off a few days."

"Then what?"

"I don't know! Christ, how did I get into this?"

"Lot, call me right after you talk to him, okay? We'll be home tonight. I can hock my engagement ring for almost $1,200. Or I could sell my Toyota, maybe get $2,000."

"Oh, Leen, I couldn't let you do that. I'll find a way out of it."

"I'd do it for you, babe."

"I know you would, but I won't let you. I'm gonna think about this and call you tonight, okay?"

Charlotte Albers replaced the receiver and inspected her slender body. Some white guys got their kicks with black girls. It was worth a try, even though she knew her price was steep. She was attractive, had a good figure and big breasts, but would he go for the deal?

A half-hour later she was dressed and had done her makeup to show off her big eyes to best effect. She wore a low-cut white dress. She hoped to hell the bait was good enough.

SHE STOOD in Jody Warren's pricey cliff-top condo overlooking the Willamette River. Warren laughed again and shook his head.

"Let me get this straight. You can't pay, but you'll give me two nights in the sack for $625 a night?"

"That's right. If you buy me, you pay what I'm worth."

"Not a chance. You owe me $1,250, and tomorrow at six it goes to $1,500. I want my money."

Jody Warren was short and fat. His face was pocked from acne. His hair was stringy, messy and long. He wore a dirty T-shirt that barely covered the big gut, white and hairless, that protruded above his tight blue jeans. His zipper was half open.

"Can you pay, Charlotte?"

"You know I can't."

"Maybe you can. You got yourself an exciting body." He petted her breasts. Charlotte gritted her teeth and held herself rigid.

"Tell you what. You want to pay off your loan getting laid, I can find two, maybe three johns a night for you. I'll shoot for $250 and sell at about $200. You earn half. In a week you should be able to work off your loan."

"As a whore?"

"You got special privileges or something? You'll work as a black call girl. You don't walk the streets."

She pulled away. His hand clawed her dress, pulling it off her shoulder.

"Not a chance." She ran for the door.

"Suit yourself. I got twelve guys who'll gang-bang you right now."

Charlotte Albers leaned against the door and slowly slid to the floor.

Warren stood over her and lifted her to her feet.

"Hey, Charlotte, sweetheart, it won't be that bad. Course you know I got to test you out first before I can offer you to my customers."

She stared through him.

"As soon as you pay off the loan, you can keep on working or quit. That's up to you." He pulled the remaining thin white strap off her shoulder and drew the white dress down to her waist. She wore no bra.

"Yeah, Charlotte, I think we'll make some money together. Come in here and we'll find out for sure."

Two hours later, Charlotte Albers sat in a bedroom on the fourteenth floor of the Rose Hotel. She was naked. A white man twice her age drank from a glass and put it on a dresser.

"Little lady, that was fine. I mean fine! Warren sure can pick good whores."

Charlotte stared at the wall.

She turned. "May I go now?"

"Go? Hell, no! We got an all-night deal here, sweetheart. We're just getting started."

She got off the bed and headed toward a doorway.

"Where you going?"

"Bathroom."

She might get paid off, but not in a week or two. It would take a year! She could never stand the humiliation.

"After I use the bathroom I'm dressing and going home," she announced. "You're a disgusting pig!"

"You shitty little slut. Nobody calls me names."

"I'm not a slut!"

"What is this, a church picnic? You sell your ass for your bread, girly."

"You've got no right...." Charlotte ran for the bathroom, and stared at her image in the mirror.

When she came out she was crying.

I'm sorry, Leen. I'm so sorry!

She opened the sliding-glass door that led to the balcony.

The man looked up at her.

She stared back for a moment, then rushed forward and dived over the railing.

3

The Executioner stared at the rain. He brushed the water from his eyes and checked the number on the modest house in the Laurelhurst section of town. Nice houses, old but well built, with good lawns. He walked up from the sidewalk and rang the bell.

Al Capezio should have known better than to answer the door himself. But he was young and still learning.

"Yeah?" he said, standing in the doorway.

Bolan grabbed his shirt, jerked him onto the dimly lit porch and pushed the muzzle of the Beretta 93-R against his temple. "Tell your wife you have to go next door and help your neighbor for a few minutes."

Capezio's eyes widened. He called the message to his wife, and Bolan closed the door.

"Who the hell are you?"

"You don't want to know, Al. We're going to your office."

Bolan pushed him toward the Thunderbird.

At the car Bolan frisked Capezio thoroughly, then shoved him across the seat to the passenger side. He got in behind the wheel.

As he drove, Bolan tossed Capezio a marksman's medal. The Mafia lieutenant examined it.

"So, you were in the Army. So what?"

"Just thought you'd enjoy thinking about it."

The Executioner drove three miles to Northeast Sandy, along it for a few blocks, then down an alley. He parked at the rear of the Eagleton Loan Company.

"Into the office, Al."

Capezio shook his head. "We never keep much cash here. Two or three thousand, tops."

"Every little bit helps, Al. Now open up."

They entered an office divided into a dozen cubicles, with a desk and a chair in each.

"So what games do we play now?" asked Capezio.

"I want names and addresses for all your loan-sharking offices like this one, and I want names and hangouts for each of your street sharks—like Leo the Fish used to be."

"Whaddya mean, 'used to be'?"

"Leo and I had a meeting tonight in his favorite bar."

"You snuffed Leo?"

"A case of lead poisoning. Now get the records for me fast, or you join him."

The mafioso dug through a desk drawer until he found what he was looking for. He handed it to Bolan. It was a computer printout. Bolan examined it and put it in his pocket. Then he demanded a list of all the cathouses Capezio operated for the Canzonaris.

Another neat computer printout went into the Executioner's pocket. Suddenly Capezio made a rash move. He whirled, grabbed a weapon from the desk and lifted it to fire. Two rounds whispered from the Beretta, pulping Capezio's heart and snuffing out his life.

A locked file cabinet was marked Loan Records. Bolan put half a cube of C-4 plastic explosive on the front of it and another on a locked file labeled diskettes. He inserted timer detonators into the soft explosive and set them for three minutes.

He was a block away when the bombs went off. So much for the loan and call-girl headquarters.

Heading downtown, Bolan stopped at a drugstore and made two photocopies of the loan-shark and whorehouse lists, put them in an envelope he bought and wrote a name on the outside.

He drove across the Morrison Street Bridge and stopped at the Portland Central Police Station. He handed the envelope to the first uniformed cop he saw.

"Could you see that Lieutenant Dunbar gets this right away? He's waiting for it."

The cop nodded and continued into the building. Bolan stopped at a restaurant and ordered coffee. Lists of targets to be eliminated were now a standard practice in Bolan's flaming war against injustice and terror. His actions against the KGB, murderers of his lover, April Rose, had been guided by a list he had seized of enemy agents working in America and the free world. Bolan made the KGB pay by working his way down that list. Now he had other kill lists to join the one that was central to the thrust of the Executioner's fight. Now he brooded on the escalation of his war, and on those who would be immediately affected by it.

Fred Dunbar. Sergeant Fred Dunbar. They had worked together in Nam for almost a year. Dunbar had been strong on the search-and-destroy missions. He tried line crossing once and almost got himself killed. Bolan and his penetration team Able found the remains of Dunbar's squad and carried them out of there.

Now Dunbar was a lieutenant in Vice in Portland, and a fine cop. Bolan checked his watch and saw that it had been a half hour since Lieutenant Dunbar should have received the goods. He went in a phone booth and called his old friend.

"Lieutenant Dunbar, Vice," the voice answered.

"I hear you do good work, Dunbar. Did you get my envelope?"

"Yes. Who is this?"

"Think you can do any good with those names and addresses? One sheet shows the Mafia-run loansharking operations. The other contains all of the Mob's cathouses. You probably know about most of them, but I thought I'd bring your records up to date."

"Who is this? The voice sounds familiar."

"Put it together, soldier. I'll be in contact. Stay hard." Bolan hung up.

CHARLEEN GRANGER SAT in her comfortable living room in an east-side condo. She was an exact copy of her sister, Charlotte Albers. She was watching a show on television, but every minute or two she glanced at the telephone on an end table. Her husband, Ed, sat across the room, reading a paperback and watching the good bits on the tube.

"Charlotte's in some kind of big money trouble," she had told her husband when he got home. They'd decided they had to let Lot try to work it out. If everything else failed they would take a signature loan at the bank to save her from the loan sharks.

Charleen could never recall Lot being so frightened as when they had talked. Lot did not cry much; she was tough, assertive and independent. But lately she had a string of bad luck.

Charleen walked to the kitchen, then wandered into the bedroom, where she hung up some clothes. She returned to the living room and dropped into a chair.

The chiming mantel clock struck eleven.

They watched the local news, then Johnny Carson.

"Lot should have called by now," Charleen said.

Ed looked up. "We'll hear. We can't live her life for her."

"I know, that's what scares me." Charleen saw Carson doing his monologue, but didn't hear the words.

THE FIRST POLICEMAN ON THE SCENE had to push people back from the grisly mess on top of the Datsun in the parking lot.

"Keep back, move it back, all the way now. This isn't a sideshow."

Another squad car pulled in, and then two more, and the police used tape to mark off the area.

Officer Quincy Smith lifted the tape for the coroner to pass. He walked with the small man in the black suit up to the bloodstained white Datsun.

The roof of the car had caved in. The black girl had been beautiful, still was. She was naked. The back of her head was crushed, but her face was perfect. He looked up and saw a dozen small balconies she could have come from. Detectives would be working those dozen rooms as quickly as they could.

It did not take the coroner long. Preliminary judgment on the cause of death: broken spinal cord and massive brain damage. Officer Smith placed a sheet over the body and motioned to the men with a stretcher.

Two ambulance attendants were bloody before they got the broken body off the Datsun and onto the stretcher.

"You were the first on the scene?" asked a plainclothesman whom Smith recognized as a detective from homicide.

"Right. I got here and waited. There were some people up on those balconies looking out, but they were just curious about the sirens, the activity."

"Any guess, Officer Smith?"

"Jumped or was pushed."

The detective grunted and marched off toward the hotel.

Detective Ormsby went directly to the sixth floor. The first five floors were too low a launching point to reach the Datsun.

Room 606 was vacant. The hotel manager met him there and they went to 706. A couple from California had occupied the room for three days. They had not noticed the disturbance.

On the next three floors they found nothing. A

man in 1106 had tried to hide a small quantity of marijuana when Ormsby came to the door, but the detective told him to forget it and they moved on. A call came for Detective Sergeant Ormsby to go up to the fourteenth.

He and the hotel manager went together. A uniformed cop showed them a woman's clothes and a purse. He had not opened it. Sergeant Ormsby did, and found a picture of a black girl about the right age and height. He looked at the face, and was sure. The girl, Charlotte Albers, had fallen or been pushed from 1406. No one was in the room. A call showed it had been rented to John Smith.

"Hooker," the hotel manager said.

"Probably," Ormsby said.

Downstairs, he found out that "John Smith" was white, about forty and had arrived alone. There was nothing left in the room to suggest he had been there. They would dust for prints, just in case.

"Any next-of-kin card?" the manager asked.

"Yes. You want to make the call?" The manager shook his head, retreating. "Figures," Ormsby said. "We'll let our police psychologist do that. He's going to earn his money tonight."

4

Mack Bolan left the restaurant, drove to his hotel, and took the elevator directly from the underground garage to the lobby. No one would leave a message at the desk for him: no one knew he was there.

He went to the bank of phones, slid into a booth, spread ten quarters in front of him, then dialed a ten-digit number. The operator asked him to deposit the toll, and he did. Then a phone in Denver rang three times. There were three clicks as his call was mechanically forwarded to another number, which rang four times and he got a local dial tone.

The dial tone came from a third number in Denver. Bolan punched in a long-distance number for Del Mar, California, and a moment later someone answered the phone.

"Yes?"

"Sentinel here, Strongbase. This phone-number latch-up you developed—you're sure there's no way it can be traced?"

"Absolutely none, guy," the younger voice said.

"How are the installations going?" asked the Executioner.

"On schedule. Today we hooked up the second on-line computer. We should be fully operational soon.

I have something you may be interested in. There's
talk about a big gunrunning operation going down
within the week. Either in Portland or San Francisco,
with the betting leaning toward the Northwest. I have
a batch of printouts from Law Enforcement Agencies' headquarters and a special briefing to all LEAs
from Justice. Maybe I should run it up there for you
to check out.''

"I want to know about it.''

"I can get a 7 A.M. flight to Portland.''

"I'll meet you at the airport. As a test, bring me
ten loaded magazines for the 93-R in your checked
luggage. You might as well stay a couple of
days. Perhaps you can do some research for me up
here.''

"I'll be there.''

"Remember, you'll be strictly backup.''

"Suits me fine.''

"See you tomorrow.''

MACK BOLAN AWOKE AT 5:30 the next morning,
donned tan slacks and a light-tan sport coat that covered the 93-R and went downstairs. At the newsstand
he bought *The Oregonian*. On the front page was an
old picture of him, as well as a sketch of him in his
blacksuit with a submachine gun and combat harness. It was a good likeness.

He returned to his room and ordered breakfast.
Then he attached a thick black mustache to his upper
lip with spirit gum, donned a pair of reflective sunglasses and a tan beret.

He completed the disguise as room service arrived.

The waiter noticed nothing unusual. Bolan consumed the toast, orange juice and coffee.

The morning paper featured a long story about Mack Bolan and described The Executioner as "a vigilante figure fighting the KGB and the Mafia, or a cold-blooded killer," depending on your point of view. It even revealed that he had apparently been dead for a year, then had turned up not dead at all but working for the government.

The story detailed that he was wanted by the FBI and the CIA as well as half a dozen foreign intelligence agencies, including the KGB.

The story concluded:

Portland Police refuse to discuss the possibility that the Executioner is in town, but the presence of marksman's medals at the triple killing yesterday and the second loan-operation blast seem to indicate that the Executioner is indeed here.

Organized Crime specialists say that both loan firms hit yesterday are known to be closely tied to the Portland Mafia.

Police say they have no warrants naming the Executioner. The FBI would not comment when asked if they have such warrants or if they are actively searching for the vigilante.

THE MENTION OF HIS NAME IN THE NEWSPAPER sent a chill down Mack Bolan's spine. Obviously it was his contact with Dunbar, the vice cop from Portland whom he'd known in Nam, that had instigated the report, and Bolan had no regrets that his message had gotten through loud and clear. But he knew that any newspaper report would be a distortion, inevitably a falsehood, just another source of future misconceptions.

The true story of Mack Bolan was too searing, too raw, too *personal*, for the pages of a newspaper. The truth of his own story continued to trouble Mack Bolan himself.

When April Rose was killed, he found himself shifting his entire psyche onto automatic pilot. And in that mode he undertook the Russian hit, the killing of a Soviet test pilot in Afghanistan after the enemy raid on Stony Man Farm in which April was shot dead. The killing of the young pilot was a decisive act for Bolan, because the man's father, Greb Strakhov, became the Executioner's sworn enemy.

The Strakhov war continued through many missions, and was still fiercely unresolved. But immediately following the tragedy at Stony Man—a complicated time for Mack Bolan—some of those missions were more harrowing, more bizarre, than others.

For a start, the Bolan invasion of Russia by way of Afghanistan necessitated the killing of a Canadian journalist, Robert Hutton, who had betrayed Bolan and who ended up as a halo of pink mist when the Executioner helped the guy drop from a helicopter onto the spinning rotors of another chopper below.

It was not a deed to endear him to the journalistic world, and indeed Bolan found himself strictly persona non grata in the America to which he returned following his covert, deadly blitz on Moscow.

U.S. politicians, agency chiefs, bureaucrats and

law-enforcement officers all suddenly found an excuse to be down on Bolan. The get-Bolan response was undoubtedly a reaction to their own fears of the big guy, a certain unease they experienced with the legend of the Executioner, a guilt over what Mack Bolan really represented.

So Bolan was very much on his own, and the difficulties mounted immediately. From the extreme and unsanctioned vengeance he wreaked in the sewer city called Washington to his twisting adventures in Kampuchea when representing the League of Families in search of American POWs lost in the blood-soaked world of the Khmer Rouge, Mack Bolan prevailed without ever knowing who his allies were—who would let him live or try to make him die.

Of course, Bolan knew who his real friends were, his true allies.... Aaron Kurtzman, the computer scientist paralyzed in the KGB smash on Stony Man Farm, who now gave secret support to Bolan with all the data resources and computing capacity it was possible to conceive of in the mid-1980s; Jack Grimaldi, the pluckiest pilot in modern history; Leo Turrin, a brilliant guy riding a desk in the Justice Department who showed up to fight alongside Bolan in the most unlikely places; Hal Brognola, the senior warrior of Stony Man along with Yakov Katzenelenbogen, and a national-security diplomat of outstanding powers who could always be relied on to get Bolan in or out of his latest fix; David McCarter, the British hero of Phoenix Force, who regularly became so transformed in the company of Mack Bolan that he achieved heights of reckless daring too hair-raising for dispatches and newspaper reports; Carl Lyons, Mr. Ironman himself, who admitted to only one equal in the world, and that was Mack Bolan. And, of course, the ghost of April Rose, because a phantom of incomparable beauty and courage was as much a friend as he could hope for in a time and a world of irreparable bereavement.

And so many others...Able Team, Phoenix Force, Nile Barrabas of the Soldiers of Barrabas, many extraordinary and powerful men and equally magnificent women, who transformed his recent life from one of shadows to a career of flaming glory once again.

His revival owed everything to the sweetness and the rock hardness of real people who knew him well and would serve him until death; it was that kind of loyalty. He was proud to fight with such allies.

And now, on top of all else, his own resurrection was shared by that of his kid brother, Johnny, survivor of the holocaust that had once struck Bolan's family. Johnny was a young man in his early twenties, raised by adoptive parents, who today lived and breathed Mack Bolan as if his elder brother were himself.

Bolan had a message for Johnny: no buddies.

One day Mack Bolan would explain to Johnny Bolan Gray why it was that he believed that.

On such a day he would explain why something called the Council of Kings had everything to do with that belief.

He would reveal who actually sat on the Council of Kings, and would demonstrate how a thing that sounded so Mob-like, so criminal in the parochial world of Portland, did in fact have its origins in Vietnam.

Unforgettably, Bolan had a buddy called Buddy back in Nam.... Hell yes, he knew about the buddy system. And what destroyed it. He knew all about the goddamned bloodsuckers, the destroyers of humanity called the Council of Kings.

One day he would tell Johnny what possessed him about that group of evil powermongers. One day he would tell his young brother about Buddy. To Bolan's mind the Council, back in those Vietnam days, was more evil than all the Mafia families currently being rounded up in New York City by Justice and the NYPD. No recent mob council could be as vile as the original one that lorded over a jungle land ravaged by a thousand years of foreign kings, and Bolan would eventually get even with everyone who was part of it. That was what motivated him this very day: to strike at those who perverted the word "family."

But first Mack Bolan had business to conduct. Mob business. Only execution could await the body-cocks who cut into Sergeant Mercy's path even as he tried to cope with the unjust deaths of all his lovers and friends and as he imperiled his own sanity with grief-stricken visions of April Rose, lost forever. But he would not ever imperil the fight itself. Vietnam... the Mafia miles...the terrorist wars...now back to mopping up the Mob—the same goddamned ever-lasting war, and it throbbed through Bolan's being like the living, palpitating memory of all the dead whom he loved.

Ah, death, it was indeed the Executioner's very life itself.

One day he'd explain to Johnny how it had all come to this, and he hoped to heaven the young guy would understand.

For the kid's sake.

Johnny's survival would depend on it.

DISGUISED, THE EXECUTIONER LEFT THE HOTEL and toured two more possible loansharking hits, then drove to the north side of Portland, to Portland International Airport.

The 9:55 flight arrived ten minutes late. Johnny Bolan Gray marched down the ramp wearing a tie and jacket and carrying a briefcase. These two Bolans, one half the age of the other, both branded by the same vigilante cause, were now together in the middle of the heat, dead center in the limelight as the local media brought the Executioner story right up to date. Mack Bolan decided to risk it nevertheless. He knew that role camouflage could serve as well defensively as offensively, and he put that into play. Right now he was just a guy in Portland, Oregon, who was meeting his brother. Maybe some business deal, or just family business. Nothing of note.

Johnny glanced at his brother without recognizing him, looked away, then looked back and smiled. The Executioner showed the kid the front of the morning paper.

"Sounds as if you've been busy," Johnny said. "Shall we go to your hotel? I've got a bundle of material for you."

At the hotel, Johnny took a room on the same floor, then showed Mack what he had brought.

"The LEA report on the gunrunners came over the computer late last night." He handed Mack a sheaf of printouts.

"I've got a printout from Justice on the Portland Organized Crime Task Force. They list the Canzonari family and all of its businesses. There's some information about a gun store that seems so clean and legal and aboveboard they think it must be dealing in illegal arms somehow. That's about it."

Bolan turned to an inside page of the morning newspaper and folded it back. He looked at the picture of the black girl and another of the battered roof of a Datsun in a parking lot.

"Last night this woman jumped from a fourteenth-floor window. Her sister's quoted as saying that the girl was in financial trouble, may have been involved with loan sharks." Bolan glanced briefly at Johnny as he spoke.

Johnny nodded slowly. "I'll look into it."

Bolan examined the LEA reports on the guns. The texts boiled down to one grisly truth: a huge shipment of arms was heading for the West Coast, possibly camouflaged as industrial machinery. It was thought to be arriving between the twelfth and the fourteenth. Today was the tenth. It was believed that a ship, of Japanese registry, would be carrying small arms of all kinds, machine guns and submachine guns, small mortars, hand grenades and LAW rockets and launchers—enough of an arsenal to wage a small war.

The LEA spokesman feared the guns would be handled by one of the West Coast families, making available fully automatic rifles and submachine guns to every Mafia soldier in America. The rest of the weaponry might go to terrorists training somewhere in the continental United States.

"Let's get moving. You try to find this woman in the paper, the sister of the dead girl, and I'll check out that gun store."

An hour later Bolan was standing outside a gun shop on the east side near the approaches to Ross Island Bridge. The sign over the door said Northwest Guns, Inc., and in smaller lettering, Firearms of all types, Loading Equipment, Camping Gear, Surplus. It was the kind of store Mack Bolan could get lost in. It displayed a dizzying assortment of weapons: air guns, fancy target pistols, Uzis, Ingrams and others that he hadn't even heard of.

He talked to a clerk and moved on. Nowhere did he detect any kind of weapon or even a round that was not legal.

In the back corner he found an armorer repairing guns and rifles. The man had a small machine shop and could make parts.

The only problem with the store as a whole was proportion. It was built inside a warehouse. When Bolan went outside, he realized the exterior was almost twice as large as the shop within. That left one hell of a lot of room for storage. He would check that out later.

The Executioner drove past one of the brothels on

the list. He watched two cars turn into a parking lot in the back. Bolan parked in the street. Nobody could see the customers entering through the front. Another car rolled into the lot. If the brothel had this much business in an afternoon, it must be roaring at night.

Bolan found a phone and called the Portland Central Police Station. He reached Lieutenant Dunbar.

"Dunbar, I just drove past a whorehouse. It's still in operation. Why?"

"Hey, guy, we got other things to do besides bust hookers. Like a girl who took a leap out of a fourteenth-story window. Besides, we closed down three houses last night. Any idea what it does to booking when we bring in fifteen girls and about twenty johns? It raises hell with the whole operation."

"So you want *me* to raise hell in this town? Work on it, guy."

Bolan hung up and drove away. As he neared the hotel, he wondered about the gun shipments. How could you fool the port customs officials that guns were really industrial machinery? They must have a system. Big bucks under the table? It would be interesting to find out.

5

A Cadillac limo swept uphill through Washington Park, curved along Southwest Fairview Boulevard and turned into a large estate overlooking the park and two-thirds of Portland.

Don Gino Canzonari's personal bulletproof crew wagon swung to the rear of the house and the four-car garage. The driver bailed out quickly and opened the rear door for a tall muscular man. He was clean shaven, with dark, piercing eyes, and moved like an athlete. He was a Black Ace, the only man Don Canzonari had ever known who carried a hit specialist from *La Commissione*'s elite corps.

Vince Carboni stepped out of the Caddy and looked at the backyard of the Canzonari-family headquarters. Three acres of lawns and gardens trailed slightly upward toward a mass of evergreen trees. Carboni didn't care that he couldn't tell one tree from another. He was a city boy born and bred, and he was proud of it. He straightened the jacket of his seven-hundred-dollar suit and stepped along the sidewalk in his two-hundred-dollar Italian imported shoes. Everything was so green he could not believe it.

Carboni ignored the beauty, the strangeness. He was there on business.

"Where?" he asked curtly.

"Right this way, Mr. Carboni. Mr. Canzonari is waiting for you."

Carboni swept past the driver, who held the door, adjusting the Colt Commander under his jacket.

The house was palatial, even the rear entrance, but Carboni did not notice. He would not have appreciated the cherry-wood paneling in the vestibule as he marched along, a snarl slowly taking over his face.

Gino Canzonari sat on a screened-in porch in the far wing, indulging in a breakfast of fresh orange juice and prunes. It was a little after eight in the morning.

Canzonari rose from the chair, grunting as he hoisted the 250 pounds on his five foot five frame.

"Vince! Good to see you!"

Don Canzonari had met Carboni before, and knew his reputation for being disrespectful. But he was a good hit man, the best contract specialist the Commission had. No one was better suited to take out the Executioner.

Canzonari responded to Vince Carboni's silence by saying, "The guy left a marksman's medal at the loan office where he gunned down three of my boys from a sniper spot."

"Must have used a high-powered rifle," muttered the visitor. "What else?"

"He whacked out Leo the Fish in a bar in Leo's home turf with fifty people around. Nobody knew anything had happened, thought old Fish was sleeping. Silencer, I'd guess. Took Leo's roll and his loan cards. My people are getting nervous."

"Tell them to relax. Vince Carboni is here and the Executioner has forty-eight hours to live."

"I've heard that before, Vince. Last night this madman pulls my loans director out of his own house, takes him to the company office, drills him twice, steals I don't know what and blasts the office into junk. He ruined every loan record on the premises. The bastard has cost me over a million already, and he ain't been in town for twenty-four hours."

Carboni removed his jacket, hung it over a chair and sat at the small table.

"Don Canzonari, I want a crew wagon with plenty of firepower inside. You have any automatic submachine guns?"

"One MP-40. I had it out once and it..."

Carboni held up his hand and continued.

"I need five hundred rounds and two good men. A driver and one for backup. I want your best gunner. I want him here now."

The Don nodded, made a phone call. When he hung up he made an impatient gesture.

"His name is Rocco. Damn good man."

"I'll need three .45 autos and lots of magazines. After that I'll let you know what happens."

"Right. I've got a room for you here and a hotel room downtown. You can use either or both."

An hour later Carboni had settled into his room in the Canzonari mansion. He watched a Mexican maid unpack his bags. When she was done he fieldstripped and oiled the MP-40, a weapon he had not seen for a while. This one was in good shape; like most of them it probably fired high and to the left. But he would not need to sight it in. He would just spray the target.

Once he'd checked out the weapons, had met his wheelman and inspected the car, he returned to the Portland Don.

"Where's Rocco?"

"He got hung up, but he'll be here in half an hour. Now what is the procedure?"

"The Executioner is my job. The minute he shows his nose, I want your people to call you before they take a breath. I want to know where he is. He's slippery, but with a fast-working crew we can track him down. Then he's my meat."

"I've offered five thousand dollars for the man who first spots him and reports in. What about the head money, the million the Commission put up?"

"It's still waiting to be collected," Carboni said.

"You eligible?"

"Damn right." He shrugged. "And now I find myself waiting for this great gunman, Rocco. When he gets here, keep both him and the driver in the limo. If we get a call, I want them there and the damn engine warmed up."

Canzonari returned to his desk and called his loan operators, commanding them once again to contact him immediately if they even suspected the Executioner was around.

He called in his *consigliere*, and they discussed the problem of who to put in charge of the loan and prostitution operations. It was hard to believe that Al Capezio was gone. He'd been slow to develop, but he had a good future. Now they must pick a new lieutenant.

The Don stared beyond his screened porch at the pool and acres of carefully tended lawns. He tried to enjoy the sun while he could. His was a high-risk occupation. He ought to live the good moments for all they were worth.

He had lost five good men in the past few hours. Vince Carboni must be an expert. Anybody the Commission sent would be top drawer. But was he good enough to take out Mack Bolan? Five men whacked out and not a clue for the cops or his own "rectifiers."

He phoned Joey to meet them in the study with the computer evaluations on the top men.

Don Canzonari lumbered to his feet and waddled up to his office.

Joey was there when he arrived. The *consigliere*, Joseph Morello, went to his own office for some files and returned a few minutes later.

Joey grinned at his father and slapped down computer printouts. Joey was twenty-six, a graduate of the University of Oregon at Eugene and a bona-fide computer whiz. He had set up the programs and the hardware for the entire system. Now he could call up facts and figures on any of the family businesses, legitimate or otherwise. He'd even rigged his office so that anyone sitting in a certain chair could be videotaped from one of three cameras.

"Okay, business. Who do we have with leadership qualities who isn't already assigned?" the elder Canzonari asked.

" 'Leadership'? We aren't exactly overwhelmed with top candidates." Joey picked up a printout and flipped through the pages. "Best man for the job is Frank Genaro. He's been with the family for seven years. Has served well in half a dozen shoot-outs. Wounded once. Called to testify in a court case and said all the right things for the family."

Gino looked at his lawyer, who nodded. "I didn't think of Frank, but he could do well. How much education?"

"He graduated from high school," Joey said, reading from the printout.

"Morello, you talk to him. Tell him he's got to get the whole thing together again quick. We're losing too much in interest payments. And warn him that the Executioner probably knows about every one of our outlets."

The *consigliere* nodded and left. Gino Canzonari turned to his son. "Now what about Jupiter? Is everything on schedule?"

Joey examined another printout and smiled. "Looks like it. My latest data show that the ship should be here the morning of the thirteenth, less than three days from now. The night before, we're having a little gathering of about thirty family people from up and down the coast and as far inland as the plains states. They all want to see what we have for sale."

"I don't want that hardware around any longer than necessary."

"Don't worry, dad. I figure none of the illegal stuff will be in our warehouse for more than twenty-four hours. We'll have twenty delivery trucks standing by for loading and immediate dispatch."

"And the Japanese crewmen and officers are all getting double pay for this run?"

"All taken care of. Envelopes with their cash will be in my briefcase, along with a million in cash for the man from Rome who put the shipment together. The balance we pay through our bank by computer, sending the cash to their account in Rome."

"Not a check?"

"No. Electronic banking will make the flow of money impossible to trace."

Joey left his father's office and went to the second floor, where he opened a double-locked door. He entered his computer room and settled behind his favorite machine. Then he punched up a category he had not used since creating it a year earlier.

"Mack Bolan," he requested. The screen filled with references to items in the computer's memory. He inspected the material. It all had come from a central computer in New York on a series of eight-inch disks.

Joey kept reading, astonished at what this man now threatening the Canzonaris had done in the past.

6

Mack Bolan pulled the Thunderbird to the curb. He wanted to return to the gun store and look inside, but that was nighttime work.

He made a U-turn and drove back toward the store, circled the block and looked for an alley. There was none, but he found a vacant lot that gave him a distant but good view of the back of the store.

From his vantage point he could see the loading dock and the wide roll-up door. Then he slid down in the seat, stretched out his legs and played a waiting game. A pickup pulled up to the dock, loaded with two crates.

Bolan figured they could be legitimate goods bound for a gun club or a shooting range. The driver did not enter the building. There was a small hut attached to the warehouse, where a man filled out papers and serviced clients.

One more truck used the dock in the next hour. Bolan drove to a nearby phone booth and tried Johnny's room at the hotel. There was no answer. He did not leave a message, but returned to the vacant lot.

Big signs at the retail gun store listed its hours as eight to five, and Bolan hoped that covered the warehouse section. At 5:15 P.M., he locked the Thunderbird and walked through the deserted lot, across a dirt track and toward the rear of Northwest Guns, Inc.

Fifty feet from the back door he paused behind some brush. A blacktop circled the building and became a parking lot, probably for employees and delivery trucks. No rigs were in the lot.

Clouds had been darkening overhead all day, and as he moved forward again, rain came down in a steady drizzle. Bolan ran for the small shed by the loading dock and checked the hut. Empty.

He tried the small door beside the roll-up: locked. There were no windows. He dug out his lock picks and worked over the tumblers for a minute. Then he tried it and the latch slipped free. The Executioner eased the door open slowly. It was dark inside. He slid in, turning the knob on the night latch so the lock engaged as he closed the door.

He took out his pencil flash and flicked it on. He was in a warehouse with twelve-foot shelves only partly filled. He checked the first series of shelves and found a box with four Uzi submachine guns. They were fully automatic, with overhung bolts and 32-round magazines.

The next rack showed a pair of familiar M-16 rifles. They were fully automatic, not the semiautos civilians can legally own.

So the store was a front; the big money was in the back shop, where the Mafia stored illegal arms it could sell to whoever had cash to buy them.

Bolan heard a door creak open, and he dodged behind a stack of crates just as a pair of overhead floodlights came on. It was not the full set of lights, for which Bolan was thankful. Crouching low, he saw a night watchman with a key box in his belt. Bolan relaxed. The guard was making his rounds.

The watchman strolled to both sides of the dimly lit warehouse and evidently used keys there, then returned to the door through which he had entered. He extinguished the lights and continued into another section of the building.

The Executioner had seen what he wanted to. He picked up one of the Uzis, put four loaded 32-round magazines inside his shirt and headed for the back door. He might as well restock his own arsenal while he was there.

The nightstalker slid out the rear door, heard the lock snap into place and walked in the rain to his Thunderbird. There was no one around to observe the drenched figure in the twilight.

It was time to chat with Lieutenant Dunbar about the arms shipment. As one of the Law Enforcement Agencies that received briefings, the PPD might have some late information to share. Bolan stopped at a phone booth in a filling station and called Dunbar.

The detective answered.

Bolan did not identify himself, just asked a question. "What do you know about a large shipment of illegal weapons headed for the West Coast right now?"

Dunbar knew the voice. "Nothing. Are the arms coming in here?"

"What I heard. Don't your people read their LEA notices?"

"I never see them."

Mack hung up, suddenly tired. He drove to his hotel on the west side, flopped on the bed and did not hear the phone when it rang four times about midnight.

AT SIX A.M. MACK BOLAN WAS SITTING in his rented Thunderbird across from Northwest Guns, Inc., watching the parking spot labeled Reserved—Manager.

It had stopped raining. Gray clouds still moved overhead on their way to eastern Oregon and Idaho.

Bolan left his car and jogged to the Cadillac that was pulling into the reserved spot. He leaned both hands against the door and stared at the small man behind the wheel. He was about forty, and a touch of fear flamed in his eyes as he looked up.

"You the manager?"

"Yes. Nate Enright. May I get out?"

"Yeah, sure." Bolan backed up, playing the country bumpkin.

"What can I do for you?"

"Fire-insurance investigator. Need to look around. See if you sell black powder, how you handle it, the usual."

"We just sent our policy payment in."

"Right, but our new corporate owner has made some changes. I'm sure you know how that is."

"No, I don't know how it is. The insurance agent is my brother. His company has not changed hands. You're lying about this whole insurance scam."

"Who owns the gun shop?"

"I do."

"You run the warehouse in back of your store?"

"No, I rent the front half of the building."

"Who do you rent from?"

"Northwest Warehouses, Incorporated, a local outfit."

"Which is owned by Gino Canzonari."

"So?"

"You don't know who he is?"

"Never met him. I hear he's associated with organized crime. But that doesn't paint me with the same stripes. Now if you'll excuse me, I have work to do."

"I'm sorry for any inconvenience. My mistake."

"No problem."

Enright marched off to the front door, where two employees were waiting.

No wonder the front part of the store looked so damn legal. It was! Bolan checked the time. A little after six. At the phone booth down the block he called Johnny.

"I'll be there in fifteen minutes."

Mack hung up and wheeled the Thunderbird downtown.

THE EXECUTIONER DID NOT INTEND to make mistakes. In his occupation, they meant death. Bolan had learned this early in Vietnam.

It was in Nam that he was nicknamed "Executioner," and the name clung to him as his kill total mounted and he became known and respected from the Mekong Delta to Hanoi.

The other side of the Executioner was not so well-known. The common people of Vietnam, caught between a grinding war machine and the desire to live at peace, often found this Executioner to be a merciful friend.

He put his own life in danger time after time to rescue children and women in the line of fire. To these people he became known as Sergeant Mercy.

Bolan found no contradictions in the two labels. He did each part of his job with equal determination.

He performed his duty as he saw it, and was proud of the job he did. Until that terrible tragedy that yanked him from the jungle and thrust him on a plane with an emergency leave in his pocket, to return home to find the members of his family either dead or hospitalized.

Bolan discovered the reason behind his family's tragedy and at once began to set the matter right. His first engagement was the Mafia loan sharks in his hometown, Pittsfield. Soon Mob families all over the country were feeling the Executioner's wrath as he utilized all his skill from the Southeast Asian hellground.

Bolan had fought thirty-eight campaigns against the Mafia when, to the consternation and embarrassment of the U.S. at not being able to control this rampaging tiger, the President issued a pardon. After Bolan's war wagon flamed out in Central Park, Bolan was presumed "dead." Secretly he rose again from the ashes as Colonel John Phoenix, working under government sanction.

This time the new enemy was terrorism.

Eventually he was framed by the KGB for a political murder in Europe, then hounded by his own government, which had fallen for the frame. A mole in the U.S. intelligence operation facilitated a KGB-sponsored attack on Bolan's command center, Stony Man Farm. The assault led to the death of April Rose, Bolan's true love.

Bolan struck at the heart of Mother Russia even as the United States and friendly nations searched for him. In one climactic showdown, he fingered and executed the mole in front of the U.S. President.

By his action, he had broken sanction. He was alone again.

Now the KGB, the CIA and police everywhere searched for the Executioner, hoping to haul him in because of the outrageous success of his vigilante actions.

Now another force was looking for him as well: the Mafia, and they put cash behind their search.

One million dollars for Bolan's head. . . .

The vigilante was scaring the hell out of evil once again!

7

The Executioner knocked on his brother's hotel-room door, then tried the handle. It was unlocked. He pushed the door open and entered. A pretty black woman was wagging a finger at Johnny as she talked. Johnny stood listening, dressed in pajama pants with no shirt. An electric shaver was in his hand and an embarrassed expression was on his face.

"Hey, the boss is here. He's the man you should talk to."

The girl turned, and Bolan saw that she was beautiful. She wore a single gold chain around her neck, conservative makeup, a jungle-green blouse and a lighter-green skirt. She stared at Bolan, and something like recognition came into her face. She said, "This young man came around yesterday asking me a lot of questions about my sister Charlotte Albers, and right away I got to thinking that he was asking questions no real reporter or writer would want to know. Can you tell me what is going on?"

Bolan moved forward, his hand out. "I'm sorry about your sister. You look exactly like her."

"'Exactly' is the right word. We are—were—identical twins."

The woman stared again at Bolan, who still wore

the mustache. He had taken off the dark glasses. Her hand flew to her mouth.

"My God! You're the one on the front page of the paper yesterday. The Executioner!"

"Mrs. Granger, you are safe. We are trying to find out if your sister was involved with a loan shark."

"You kill people. You shot those three men yesterday."

She sat down on the bed. Bolan stepped in front of her. "Did Charlotte borrow money from a loan shark?"

"Yes, she sure did. They were the ones that killed her!"

She told them about the phone call, Charlotte's need for money, even the name of the man she went to see.

"I believe in an eye for an eye," she added slowly. "I think you should do your thing."

"First, tell me the name of the loan operation."

"No, not unless you let me go along and help."

Twenty minutes later they were driving in her car down a street that showed mostly black faces.

"This block, halfway down," said the woman. They circled and came up in an alley.

Around the back of the King Finance Company was a small sign. The door was locked. Bolan used a credit card to open the door.

No one was in the room. It was filled with boxes of paper forms, an old desk and a secretary's chair with one caster missing. They slipped into the room, and Bolan unleathered the Beretta as he moved to the connecting door. They could hear voices in the next room.

Bolan opened the door a crack. He saw a short hall, a front counter and offices on both sides. Two men stood talking at the counter.

The Executioner motioned the woman to enter first. "Let's see how they react," he whispered. "We'll be behind you, watching."

Charleen Granger walked inside. The men turned and looked at her.

The first one to react was the taller man. His eyes widened, and his mouth fell open.

"Holy shit! We got a ghost!"

The second man stared at the black woman without reaction. "No ghost. Her cousin or sister, maybe." He took a step toward her. "What do you want?"

"I want to see both of you frying in hell!" She darted forward, a switchblade snapping open in her hand as she lunged the last few feet. The shorter man swept his arm out, took a cut on it, then slapped the weapon from her hand.

The taller man grabbed her and held on. "Hell, Harry, what we going to do now?" he asked.

"You're going to let go of the lady," the Executioner said as he stepped into the room, the silenced 93-R tracking them.

"Who are you, asshole?" the shorter one asked, reaching below the counter. Bolan only had time to see the twin snouts of a 12-gauge shotgun before he fired. The slug tore into the man's chest, slamming him lifeless against the wall.

The Executioner saw more movement. Another 9mm stinger from the Beretta cored the taller guy's brain, punching him backward and leaving his body draped over the counter.

The Executioner looked at the two corpses, then motioned Johnny and the woman to follow him. They left the way they came in, then got into Charleen's car and drove out to the street.

BEHIND THEM IN THE ALLEY a black man with a full beard looked up from a blanket of newspapers and yawned. He locked his eyes on the license plate, memorized it and shuffled into the back door of the loan office. What were two honkies doing with that cute black chick? That license-plate number should be worth at least two bottles of wine.

He went inside and placed a call to Jody Warren.

8

Half a mile from the loan office, Charleen Granger pulled the car over, leaned out the window and vomited, retching again and again until her stomach was empty. She transferred to the back seat and curled herself into a ball.

Bolan drove downtown to the hotel and parked outside.

"Can I drive you home, Mrs. Granger?" Johnny asked. "I'll be glad to take you there and get a taxi back."

She nodded. "If you would. I haven't ever seen anything like what I saw today."

Bolan left the car. "I'll call your room when I'm clear. There's a big loan setup I need to check out. In fact I want to double-check this one."

The Executioner looked in the side window. "Charleen, I hope you won't be talking to anyone concerning my work here."

She half smiled. "Don't worry. Anything you can do to those loan sharks has my blessing, the police be damned."

She waved, and Bolan walked quickly into the hotel, his raincoat covering the hardware. He went directly to the garage and found his Thunderbird.

Johnny drove Charleen Granger home in her car. At her insistence, he got out on a highly traveled street, where he could easily hail a cab. She waited until he had done so, then drove the few blocks home.

Johnny rode back to the hotel, went to his room and studied the computer printouts.

The more he thought about the gun store, the more it seemed there should be some tie-in. There should be somebody there who would know how to get his hands on an illegal weapon.

Johnny went downstairs, caught a cab, rode to Northwest Guns, Inc. and walked inside.

He wandered around the store for a few minutes, then approached a clerk.

"You've got a lot of fine equipment here, but I'm looking for something a little more automatic. Can you help me?"

The clerk was in his midtwenties, with hair almost to his shoulders and tied in a ponytail.

The guy squinted and rubbed his nose. "We got semiauto weapons, like the Uzi and the M-16. You planning on starting a war?" He grinned.

Johnny grinned back. "Exactly. What I'd like to get are some fully auto M-16s like the Army uses."

"Illegal as hell," the clerk said.

"Illegal doesn't bother me. And I'm not from the feds. Look, some of you guys must have a contact who knows where I can find some."

The salesman looked around; no one else was near. "Hold it down, guy. Just look around for a clerk named Emmett. He's here somewhere."

Johnny found Emmett at the back of the store, polishing a glass counter containing the most expensive guns. There were Uzis and some H&Ks and even a Weatherby Mark V rifle. Johnny explained to Emmett what he was after.

Emmett, who was about thirty and had a trim beard and flattop haircut, took a semiauto Uzi out of the display rack. "You ain't asking for much, buddy, you know that? What you need them for?"

"That's my business. I need a lot, say a sample order of a hundred M-16s fully auto, including ammo."

"You're talking big money, man, at least sixty to seventy thousand dollars!"

"You've got to spend money to make money. You have a contact I can talk to? I'm in a hurry."

Emmett scratched his head, stroked his beard and developed a small tic under his left eye. He inhaled deeply and nodded. "Hell, why not. Just don't say who told you. See a guy named Joey down at Portland General Accounting. Tell him what you need. If anybody can supply it, he can."

Johnny slid the man a twenty-dollar bill and left. Portland General Accounting—the name was fuzzily familiar. From a pocket, he took a list of Oregon firms thought by one LEA report to be associated with or owned by the Gino Canzonari family. Portland General Accounting was one of them.

Johnny caught a cab to a plush high rise downtown. Portland General Accounting took up half the seventh floor. A reception desk in the lobby led into their end of the hall. Johnny spoke briefly to the receptionist, and a tall, heavy-set man came out who looked one hundred percent gorilla.

They went down a hall and into a bare room.

"Got to frisk you," the beast said. "Boss's rules."

Johnny lifted his arms to let the man pat him down.

Satisfied, the beast grunted and waved Johnny on to the next room. Within the fancy office with modern decor and rock-band posters on the wall stood a man about Johnny's age. He was five foot ten, slight, with auburn hair that looked dyed and a clean-shaven baby face.

Johnny stared, perplexed. "I'm looking for someone who can tell me about the availability of fully automatic weapons."

"You have the right man." Joey completed a computer operation on a terminal behind him, removed a diskette from the drive and put it in his desk drawer. "What do I call you?"

"Today I'm Jim Smith. My needs are simple—one hundred M-16 fully automatic rifles. The same ones the GIs use."

Joey sat in his executive-type leather chair and leaned back.

"You're serious. Who told you I could help?"

"He said not to tell you. And yes, I'm serious. I need these weapons quickly. I understand the going price is about six hundred each."

"Could be. I'm just an accountant."

"Sure, and my real name is Jim Smith. Can we talk business, or do I find someone else?"

The lighting seemed unusually bright, Johnny noticed.

"If you can deliver the one hundred," he continued, "I'll pay you half in advance for five hundred more, along with five hundred thousand rounds of ammunition and support magazines."

"Would a foreign delivery be satisfactory?"

"Of course. I just need to be sure of the quality of the product."

Joey pushed a button on the side of the desk, then stood and paced around the room.

"Let's leave it this way," he said at last. "If I can help you, I'll know within forty-eight hours. Where do I contact you?"

"You don't," Johnny said. "I'll phone you here, and we'll meet again."

Joey smiled. "I admire a cautious man. Incidentally, Emmett called and said you might drop by. Now I have some work to do. I'll look forward to your call."

Johnny left by the door he had entered.

When the second door beyond his office closed, Joey pulled out a desk drawer and adjusted several knobs on a small control panel there. A television screen flipped up on his desk. He pushed a switch and a videotape began rolling in a Betamax.

Johnny Bolan's likeness appeared on the screen in profile. Joey froze the image and forwarded it to a set of computer memory banks for scanning and matching.

A few moments later the screen changed and the results were shown:

No EXACT MATCH. Two SIMILAR CLASSIFICATION CHOICES.

The screen then showed a picture of a young television actor whose face resembled Johnny's. A coincidence. Joey hit the delete button and the screen went blank. Then another profile came up. It was the Executioner.

Joey laughed. He studied a split screen of the two profiles, first in line sketches, then with the best photograph they had of the Executioner. There were some similarities, but a dozen or so differences. Again, a coincidence. He hit the CONTINUE button and the computer reported:

NO EXACT MATCH ON SCREEN IMAGE. NOT A KNOWN FIGURE IN ANY OF THE IDENT BANKS. NOT A FRIENDLY. NOT A COPY WITH ANY LEA MEMBER ON FILE.

Joey touched a button and the screen recessed neatly into his desk. He touched another.

"Yes, Mr. Canzonari?" asked a voice through a small speaker.

"How many tails on the man who just left my office?"

"Two."

"Good. Get a report back to me as soon as you can."

"Yes, Mr. Canzonari."

JOHNNY SENSED HE WAS BEING FOLLOWED even before he left the building.

He caught a cab, saw a tall man in a brown suit grab the next cab in line. He told the driver to take him to the airport, then asked for the police station instead. When they arrived Johnny said he now wanted to go to his hotel.

The cabby was getting curious.

"Someone's following us," Johnny said.

"Not for long!" the cabby replied. He gunned the Chevy down the block, into an alley, around the block and into the alley again. He parked behind a bakery. Five minutes later he eased out the other end of the alley and drove Johnny to the hotel. Johnny gave him a ten-dollar tip.

There was a message in Johnny's box with his key, listing a number to call. Johnny hurried to a pay phone and dialed. It was the number Charleen Granger had given him to use in an emergency.

Someone answered on the first ring.

"Yes, hello!"

"This is Johnny. I had a message to call this number."

"Thanks. I met you last night when you talked to Charleen about her sister. I'm her husband." There was a catch in his voice.

"Is something wrong?"

"Charleen has been kidnapped. There was a note on the front door. It said not to go to the police or to tell anyone, and I would be notified in six hours about ransom. We don't have any money!"

"Mr. Granger, I'm sorry. It's the same people who hurt Charlotte. Stay there. Wait for their call. I'll talk to a friend and get back to you."

After Johnny hung up, he realized he had no way to contact Mack. A chill darted through him. He had once been involved in a Mafia kidnapping in San Diego, and his lady, Sandy Darlow, had been killed. Who else would want to kidnap Charleen except the Mafia?

Johnny hurried to his room. As he waited, he paced up and down, staring at the phone, demanding that it ring.

Until it did, he could only worry.

Time and again a terrible scene returned to his mind. It was what he had seen when Sandy Darlow lay on that stainless-steel table in the garage in San Diego.

What he had seen was turkey meat.

9

Bolan powered the Thunderbird from the underground hotel garage and swept out of Portland on Southwest MacAdam Avenue, which turned into Riverside Drive and followed the Willamette River south.

He drove upstream until he came to Lake Oswego, a town as well as a lake about two and a half miles long, developed as a showplace for luxurious waterfront homes with docks.

The Executioner was interested in talking to Tony Pagano. He had never met Tall Tony. His intel indicated that in this posh community Pagano now headed a branch office for the Canzonari family.

It was not nickel-and-dime stuff. Here the trade was for ten to fifty thou. Rich people needed loans more often than the poor, and their credit was usually better. If one of them got in over his head, he went to his old man or his rich girlfriend and tapped them for the cash to prevent a scandal. Loansharking had been here for years.

Regardless of the affluence of the loan shark's victims in a place like Lake Oswego, Bolan had sworn long ago that he would remove every vestige of the Mob's loansharking operations from the face of the earth. The shark's customers might even resent it, but Mack Bolan's juggernaut of justice, out to avenge his and Johnny's family that had been so savagely victimized in the Vietnam war era, could not be stopped. The place must be hit. And the neighborhood had just better watch out for itself.

Bolan stopped at a new office building near the east end of the lake, just off State Street. The Lake Oswego Loan and Trust Company, as the name plaque identified it, was a sleek and modern building with an all-glass front, curves instead of corners, a revolving door and modern sculptures outside and in the lobby. The lawn had been manicured within a blade of its life—every green shoot was properly clipped and trimmed.

The big man in the beret and black-rimmed glasses paused inside the front door and shook the rain from his raincoat, which covered the hardware he carried.

He walked to a reception area, sinking halfway to his ankles in red plush carpet, his eyes meeting those of a tall redhead who rose behind her desk and smiled. He stopped in front of her.

"Good afternoon," she said. "How may I help you?"

"I understand Mr. Pagano is in today. I don't have an appointment but it's urgent that I see him."

"That might be difficult." She smiled, lighting her face with a special radiance that seemed to imply she was on his side. She sat behind the desk and motioned for him to sit. When he did, she punched a series of buttons on a telephone console.

She spoke softly, then turned to Bolan. "His appointment secretary wants to know your name and the nature of your business."

"My name is Mack Scott. My business is old friends. I'm like a member of the family. Tell him we have a mutual acquaintance, Freddie Gambella."

She turned back to the phone. When her eyes found him again, a touch of surprise was on her pretty face.

"Marci says you can go right in. Her door is right over there, the second on the left down the main hall."

"Thanks."

"A pleasure, Mr. Scott. Anytime."

Bolan approached the main hall; the carpet below his feet graduated from red to dark blue. He entered the second doorway on the left.

The office was an interior decorator's dream, with subdued lighting, old-master prints in expensive frames on the walls and a typewriter and computer on the secretary's pedestal desk of glass and plastic.

The secretary's blond hair was pulled back in a severe bun. Her dress was sleek and tight, highlighting her subtle curves. She wore a lot of makeup and stared vacantly in his direction. "Mr. Pagano is extremely interested in seeing you. He was a friend of Mr. Gambella, as you know. He's busy on the phone at the moment. Can I get you a drink while you wait?"

"Coffee, please."

She brought him a cup from a fancy vacuum coffeepot. The brew seared his lips. Before it was cool enough to drink, a door swung open and a tall, thin man appeared. His face was little more than skin and bone. Bolan could not remember seeing deeper-set eyes. Small blue veins showed through the tissuelike parchment covering his features as the deadly black eyes swept over Bolan.

"You said you were a friend of Freddie Gambella's?" The voice was accusing. It was the sound of death squeezed through a reedy clarinet.

"Hey, I met him couple of times. Maybe not like a friend. I heard you were in solid out here. Stopped by to pay my respects." Bolan's voice had a touch of Brooklyn and the eastern twang that was pure Mafia-soldier inflection.

"Come on, Scott. We need to talk." It was a command. Bolan left the coffee and followed the walking skeleton.

Tony Pagano's office was a barren cube. Everything within it was white: desk, filing cabinet, pictures, walls, even visitor's chair. In front of the white draperies on the far wall was a white couch, into which Bolan lowered himself as Pagano chose a seat behind the desk.

"If you knew Freddie, you know he died in a twisted crew wagon in New York State a few years ago. Some bastard cut him down with what the cops figured was a bazooka kind of rocket."

"Tough. But Freddie always did things with a flair."

"You connected?"

"Used to be with Manny the Mover Marcello."

"San Diego. Yeah, rough down there recently. You got a letter?"

"Manny didn't have time to write no letters."

"True."

"Hey, I'm just a soldier, wheelman, you know," Bolan said. "Nothing high up."

The living skeleton pondered this a moment, then nodded. "We're with Gino Canzonari, but my people work directly under me. Mostly loans, classy loans, nothing under ten grand and with plenty of interest. This is fat city out here."

"That's what I figured," Bolan said, dropping the mobster talk and rising from the couch. "Back away from the desk slowly, Tony."

The Executioner pulled the silenced Beretta from its shoulder leather. Pagano stared. A marksman's medal plopped on the white desk and Pagano trembled.

"The safe, Tony. Open up. Anybody ask any questions you put them down, or both of you are dead."

"Okay. Easy with the cannon."

They went through a second doorway and down a hall to a room at the side of the building. They entered. No one was inside. Bolan locked the door and motioned Pagano ahead. The tall man moved a file cabinet on wheels, to reveal a safe. He fixed his deadly stare on Bolan.

"Look, we run a clean operation here. High class. Nobody gets hurt. These rich bastards can afford the interest. We ain't broke an arm in over two years."

"The cash, Tony. Put it on the table in one of those bank bags."

Pagano obeyed.

"Fill it up. Hundreds."

When Pagano was finished, he looked up.

The Executioner shot him once in the forehead, blasting him against a wall. The deed would spare the guy the pain of the explosion to come. The slime-bucket slumped to the floor, lifeless. Working quickly, Bolan pressed one C-4 plastic explosive on the inside wall and set the timer for five minutes. He moved into the hall and set another charge there with a five-minute timer.

He returned with the bank bag to the lobby and the pretty receptionist. She saw him and smiled.

"How many people in the building?" he asked.

"Five or six, I guess."

"Notify them immediately that the place is on fire and that they must evacuate at once."

"But I don't smell any—"

"Hurry. There isn't much time."

She made the calls. When she was done, he took her hand. "Now let's head for the sidewalk."

"But my job. . ."

"Your job here is finished." He led her outside. They had just reached the edge of the manicured lawn when the first blast shook the building. Two men ran up to her, their eyes wild.

"What the hell's happening?" one of them asked.

She shook her head as the next blast sounded and the building sagged. Then the upper floor caved into the first in a shower of dust and crashing concrete blocks and timbers. When the smoke cleared, the receptionist turned to the tall handsome man—but he had disappeared.

BOLAN WENT BACK TO PORTLAND the way he had come: the Willamette River due north toward the junction with the Columbia and on to the Pacific. As he drove, the Executioner reviewed what he knew about the Canzonaris. The big family house was in Washington Heights, an exclusive area. The family owned half a dozen firms, including a trucking outfit, several small legitimate businesses that laundered ill-gotten money, several lumberyards and a sportfishing fleet that operated out of Astoria, Tillamook and Nehalem Bay. Most of their basic income was in gambling, drugs and girls.

Gino Canzonari's son Joey was a comer, and he was smart with computers. He lived in the Council Crest section, another exclusive area. Bolan had looked up the address in a roadside phone booth. To Bolan, it was ironic that the creep's address echoed the very slimiest thing about his father, the Don, which was the Council of Kings. Bolan figured a visit might be worthwhile.

Just after dark, the nightstalker was sitting in his car a few doors down the street from the Joey Canzonari residence. The big house was walled, but Bolan noticed no gate or guards or dogs. Joey blended in with his rich neighbors. No need for conspicuous security.

Except lights. Floodlights bathed the front and sides of the two-story house, and the two Mercedes in the driveway.

A half-hour after Bolan arrived, a man in his twenties left the estate in the 380 SL and drove away. Ten minutes later a woman emerged from the house and put the Mercedes 300 Diesel into the garage, opening and closing the door by remote control.

Twenty minutes later another woman left by the side door, walked to the street, and drove away in an old Chevy. The day help was leaving.

The rain had stopped. Mack shed his raincoat and sport coat, donned the combat harness over his black long-sleeved jersey, replaced the sport coat. Seeing no one on the street, he darted into the yard beside the Canzonari place, ran to the back and leaped the six-foot stone wall. In the Canzonari backyard he moved to the rear of the house and away from the lights.

It seemed too easy—the back door was unlocked. Bolan went through it into a family room. He heard a television near the front of the house. He was looking for a den or home office.

Somewhere a baby cried.

"No! Cindy! Not now!" It was a woman's frustrated cry. Hearing the woman walk toward him on the carpet, her slippers slapping against her feet, he slid between a couch and the wall. She went up some stairs. He heard her hushing a child, singing softly for a few minutes. Then she came downstairs.

"Oh, damn! It's over and I missed the ending again!" More sounds came from what he guessed was the living room. A cocktail shaker was rattled and the television channel was changed.

Bolan edged down the hall until he could see into the living room. A blond woman with a drink in her hand sat on a sofa, looking at the TV. Her dress was open. He moved back through the hall to the stairs and ascended quickly on silent feet.

He found six rooms: the master bedroom, two other bedrooms, a bathroom, a playroom, a den-office with three computers in it.

Two of the computers were up and running and connected by modems to the telephone. A printer evidently linked to the computers came to life and chattered out something on tractor-feed paper.

Bolan carefully turned on the light. He examined the computer setup more fully. He figured it duplicated a system elsewhere, so Joey could work there or at an office.

What could he take that would not be missed? This was a soft probe, and Bolan wanted to leave no clue that anyone had visited. Stealing software and data disks would be too obvious. What else?

The wastebasket. He searched it carefully, found a banana peel, several accordion-folded printouts of figures and balance sheets and some scraps of paper with scribbling on them.

One torn and crumpled sheet bore two words in pencil: *Karatsu Maru*. He put the paper in his pocket.

He returned quietly to the computers, looking for something of value. He found it. On one of the pull-out boards under the terminal were three sheets with signs, symbols and a list of phrases and numbers that looked like a code.

Determined to leave no trace of his visit, the Executioner found a blank piece of paper and a pencil and copied down twenty words and phrases and numbers. The two words he wrote at the top of the sheet spelled good news. They were: "Access Codes."

Finally Bolan copied the phone number on the handset near the modem and put the paper in his pocket.

Then the baby cried again.

Bolan snapped off the light as footsteps sounded on the stairs. The woman was muttering, "Second damn show you've ruined, kid." She paused outside the den, and Mack ducked behind the big desk.

The woman took two steps into the room, still muttering. "I thought this door was closed." She shut it solidly and continued down the hall.

The Executioner went to the door and listened. Nothing was audible through the solid wood; no hollow doors in this house. He waited five minutes, and at last heard faint humming as the woman returned along the hall and, he hoped, downstairs.

He opened the door slightly and looked out, saw an empty hall. He edged into the hall. Safe so far.

He was halfway down the stairs when a blond woman, naked but for blue panties, started upward from below. She was carrying a tall glass containing a small amount of clear liquid, and her eyes were only half-open. She saw Bolan and shrugged.

"Hell, Joey, when did you get home?" She climbed the steps, pecked his cheek and continued upward. "I'm crashed, Joey, smashed and bashed and skunk drunk. Don't you ever tell mom." She stumbled on the top step and slid to the carpet.

Bolan quickly went downstairs, out the door in the family room and over the wall.

TWENTY MINUTES LATER Bolan sank into a chair in his hotel room and called Johnny.

"Mack! I've been trying to get you all afternoon. Charleen Granger was kidnapped this morning—her husband called me. They said they would phone him, but he hasn't contacted me again."

"Can you come to my room?"

"Be right there."

When he arrived, Johnny told Mack Bolan all he knew about the kidnapping. "The only thing I can figure is that somebody spotted Charleen's car when we left that loan agency."

"Which is bad," the Executioner said. "Call her husband and see if he's heard anything more."

Johnny did, then shook his head. "The poor guy is still waiting."

"So we have to wait. In the meantime, see what you can do with these." He handed Johnny the sheet listing the access codes. "Did you bring your portable computer with the built-in modem?"

"I'll get it. It's in my room." Johnny Bolan fetched it, plugged it in and positioned the handset. He dialed the number to Joey Canzonari's home office and made the connection.

Johnny entered one of the codes, and the screen showed the files and subject listings each contained. Quickly he worked through a mass of bookkeeping data, then came to the intriguing code name, "Jupiter." He punched it up and whistled.

"Here it is, Mack. Look at this. A ship named the *Karatsu Maru* is due here about 1330 hours on the thirteenth. That's tomorrow! It's to come in at

Terminal One, berth fifteen. She has 9,783 metric tons, and the load is industrial machinery. Owner is listed as Canzonari Lines.''

"Paydirt," Bolan grunted. "Now we have something solid. I'll meet them upstream. But first a couple of unfinished projects. You wait for word from Mr. Granger. I've got a date in back of that gun store."

THE EXECUTIONER PUT A QUARTER OF A BLOCK of C-4 plastique against the small door of the warehouse behind Northwest Guns, Inc., and set the timer for thirty seconds. It blew the door halfway through the warehouse and started dogs howling for half a mile.

Bolan threw two smoke grenades into the building and dropped a white phosphorus grenade outside. He sprinted to the phone booth on the street that ran by the vacant lot behind the warehouse. He reported the explosion and fire to the police.

Bolan watched from the vacant lot. A few minutes later two police cars arrived, followed by a fire truck that pulled up and doused the last flames of the white phosphorus with foam. Then the police and fire inspectors toured the warehouse, and six more squad cars and two unmarked cars arrived. Bolan, deep in the shadows once again, surveyed the distant scene. That was one illegal arms dealer out of business for good. And the legitimate gun store would not be damaged by smoke or minor flames, so quick was the fire department's response to his call.

He moved on to another phone booth and called Johnny. Yes, Granger had phoned. The kidnappers had ordered Granger to bring either a hundred thousand dollars or Bolan the Bastard to a meeting set for midnight, only half an hour away. Johnny gave Mack the exact location and Mack gave Johnny some brotherly advice: stay in the hotel.

"The kidnappers know about us," Mack Bolan warned. "They made Charleen tell everything she knew about the Executioner. That's why they knew Granger could contact us. So get out of my room and wait for me in yours. Move it!"

Bolan hung up. It was his battle now.

10

Bolan tried to beat down his terrible sense of dread and urgency as he drove across the river to Mount Tabor Park. He was to meet the kidnappers "at the top, near the rest rooms." Usually there was time to prepare a battle plan, to position his transport strategically. But it was too late for that now.

He would have to play it as it came.

He passed through the park entrance and continued up a hill along a curving road to the top. There was a parking lot and grass and trees. The rest rooms were on the far side, and he veered away from them and parked below the crest of the hill, out of sight of anyone waiting above. A dozen cars were parked along a rim lookout, filled with what he guessed were a dozen couples not paying much attention to Portland's lights spread romantically below. Bolan carried the Uzi and the silenced Beretta. On his right hip hung Big Thunder. He was as ready as he would ever be.

Bolan ran for the woods beyond the lawn. Ensuring that he was unseen, he worked slowly through the fir trees and brush toward the rest rooms. After traveling about fifty yards he saw a man behind a tree near a picnic table with a rifle beside him and a pistol in his hand.

The Executioner bellied closer. He moved another twenty yards behind cover, and in the pale light of an overhead bulb outside the rest rooms saw the mobster from fifteen feet away. Bolan tried out his stage whisper.

"Hey! Bolan the Bastard showed yet?"

The man did not turn.

"No, and get back to your damn post."

The Executioner used the silenced Beretta 93-R and drilled a hole through the soldier's head.

He watched and waited. The luminous dial of his watch showed 12:15.

Twenty yards forward, near a big Douglas fir, a figure stood and stretched. Number two. During the next five minutes, Bolan spotted numbers three, four and five. A police cruiser swung through the parking lot, throwing a spotlight on each of the cars, and one by one the smoochers in the Chevys and Datsuns started the engines and roared down the hill. The prowl car made one last circle, sweeping the hill clean.

"What the hell, he ain't coming," someone whispered.

Bolan moved closer to the rest rooms, where he could align two of the ambushers in his field of fire. He pulled down the front handle on the 93-R and fired two rounds. The closer target groaned as he died.

"Was that a silencer?" a voice asked.

The Executioner sent one round into the head of the next target. He died silently.

Two left. Bolan pulled a U.S. Army hand grenade from his combat webbing and hurled it in the direction of the remaining creeps. It hit the ground, then rolled toward a picnic table and small grill built on blocks. Bolan shielded his eyes.

The blast shattered the night. Someone screamed. Someone else began firing. Bolan rolled over and sighted the Uzi on a man behind the picnic table, trying to rise.

"I'm hit!"

Two 5-round bursts from the Uzi rattled through the night to finish him off. The corpse was thrown backward over the table onto the grill, and lay there like a human sacrifice.

The last Mafia ambusher rose from behind a log near the parking lot and fired four times into the area where the submachine gun flashes had appeared. He missed Bolan by six feet, and that cost him his life.

Bolan held the trigger down on the Uzi and hosed a double S pattern around the winking flashes of the handgun. A scream followed the roar of the chattergun. Then all was silent.

Crouching, the nightfighter ran toward the rest rooms. There was a Closed sign on the Women's. Inside, Charleen Granger was slumped in a locked cubicle, her eyes puffed up and closed and her lips swollen, obviously from a brutal beating. But that torture had only made her talk, not killed her. A small-caliber weapon had delivered the death blow. Ugly black powder burns surrounded a small purple hole on her forehead.

To Mack Bolan, the place stank of Vietnam. He had his own reasons for thinking so.

He came out running. He moved from cover to cover as he worked toward his car.

The rain began again, a sudden downpour that instantly saturated him. He knew it would ease up soon and drizzle the rest of the night. As Bolan stopped behind a Douglas fir to survey the terrain ahead, he heard a stick break thirty yards to his left, from within the thick woods.

He stayed by the tree. Nothing stirred. He heard distant sirens. A shadow deep in the gloom of the woods moved. There was no sound.

Bolan stared into the blackness. Someone in there was stalking him.

The Executioner dashed to the next large tree. A shot rang out. The flash was larger than a normal handgun's. He felt the heavy slug whir by.

Bolan cocked the hammer of Big Thunder. He glared into the darkness where he had seen the flash.

He could not find the gunman.

He evaluated his position. Police on the way. A tough opponent tracking him. His car parked where the police would soon find it. He had to get his wheels away.

Bolan ran in the opposite direction to the gunman, counting on the huge tree to mask his retreat.

Hard running brought him to the Thunderbird. He opened it, started it and gunned it down the hill without headlights.

Beyond the first curves he hit the lights and took a

round through the side window. He swerved, then roared on.

The road was crooked and steep. A man could run to the bottom as fast as another could drive. The gunman would attempt to go cross-country and intercept him where the road straightened at the entrance to the park.

The Executioner accommodated him. He switched off the lights again, rolling through the now-misty rain. He judged where the runner would emerge from the brush, and stopped nearby.

Bolan sprang from the car, quietly closed the door to kill the interior light that penetrated the darkness like a million-watt beacon, and crouched as he ran to the edge of the wooded section that extended down the rear of Mount Tabor Park. He paused and listened to sounds as someone ran through the brush above, then the sounds stopped.

The Executioner held his breath.

Nothing.

A horn honked a block over. A killdeer flushed from a wet perch, sounded a plaintive cry and flew away.

There! Above in the timber a shadow slid from one big fir to the next, then was gone. The man seemed like an expert. Until he slipped. The crash was loud, less than fifty feet from Bolan. With the silenced Beretta he sent two 3-round bursts toward the sound target, but heard no response. He moved silently to the other side of the tree. He was at the edge of the woods, the attacker twenty yards within. There was no cover behind them for fifty yards to the street.

No sound came from the woods. Town noises intruded. Then Bolan rose as he heard something fall ten feet away.

Grenade. . . .

He lunged behind the tree as the bomb shattered the night. The light was brilliant, and he shut his eyes and put a hand over them. There was a shattering explosion.

Stun grenade, he guessed, turning so he could hear anyone approaching.

He heard footsteps retreating.

As his sight returned to normal, he spotted a figure running for the roadway. A black Cadillac emerged from the mist and met the runner.

The car started a three-point turn, reversing to complete the maneuver. At that moment Bolan had reached his Thunderbird below. He leaped in, ground the starter. The cars were only three or four hundred feet apart. Flames of a muzzle blast came from the enemy car. Then it vanished around a corner.

Bolan gave chase. He had to catch the man, learn his identity, kill him before he became more of a problem.

At first the route bothered Bolan. They had turned north on Sixtieth Street and then a few blocks later were on U.S. 80 North, a freeway heading east along the Columbia River. Bolan would not fire on a freeway even relatively clear of traffic. The chances of injuring passing motorists were too great. Besides, he was trying to figure the strategy of the man in the car ahead.

The odds would be two to one for a fight now, greater depending on how many Mafia soldiers were in the big Caddy. A showdown would suit Bolan just fine.

Ten miles clicked by. Bolan checked the gas gauge; almost full. He settled in behind the wheel, lulled by the rhythm of the windshield wipers. At times the road was almost at the shore of the great Columbia, then a hundred yards inland, then back to the shore.

Ten minutes later the big car swerved toward a tourist attraction called Multnomah Falls. The vehicle careered across the empty parking lot to the far side. Bolan saw the soldiers bail out of the rig.

Perhaps they saw the Thunderbird. Bolan melted into the heavy brush just past the railing inside the lot.

He crouched behind a large flat-leaf cedar and watched one man run through the parking lot unprotected, then dart into the woods.

The silenced Beretta was ready, and Bolan's jacket was open for access to the Uzi and its fresh 32-round magazine.

A car whizzed by on the road, the song of the wet tires gaining and losing a semitone as it passed.

Ahead Bolan saw a branch moving. He could see maybe twenty feet through the misty darkness.

A shadowy figure ducked under the branch and approached him. Bolan lifted the machine pistol and triggered three rounds. The shadow yelped and toppled backward. The Executioner charged through the brush, and found a trail. A wooden sign, pointing

right, read: TO THE FALLS. The trail led away from the
Mafia soldiers. Bolan followed it, climbing until he
could see the parking lot. Faint lights, security lights,
glowed at both ends.

Bolan watched the area, sectoring it the way he
used to with night vision in Nam, watching for the
smallest changes in shape or form. He saw something
move. Someone was on the trail, coming after him.
He stepped behind a big tree and waited, but the man
seemed to know he was there and came no closer.

The Executioner ran thirty yards up the trail.
Ahead he spotted a small stone bridge that spanned
the creek below the cataract. He heard the pounding
water. The falls were not wide, but were of great
height. He had read about them in tourist brochures
back at the hotel.

He stopped by the bridge and listened. Someone
moved behind him. Bolan traveled thirty feet beyond
the bridge and waited. For a minute he heard nothing
unusual. Then he heard labored breathing and saw a
man round the curve in the trail, racing toward the
bridge. The man held a handgun.

Bolan fired twice. The Mafia goon spun around
from the force of the 9mm parabellums, fell over the
parapet of the small bridge, and screamed as he
dropped twenty feet to the pool below. He floated
for a moment, then drifted downstream.

A sign beyond the bridge indicated the trail continued to the top of the falls, but warned of a three-
mile round trip. Another sign said: PARKING LOT.
Bolan deduced the trail was circular. Good. Now he
had to discover how many Mafia soldiers had been in

the Caddy. He doubted that either of the dead soldiers behind him had been the gunman who had fired at him from the car. They had been too careless.

Bolan neared the parking lot without seeing any movement. He crouched near a big tree and waited.

The roar of a big handgun took him by surprise, and as he dived he felt the bullet burn through the shoulder strap of his combat harness. It did not draw blood as it slammed past him into the brush.

The flash had appeared ahead to the left, but the man would not have lingered. Bolan moved to the two-foot log that bordered the parking lot. The crew wagon was to his right, the Thunderbird to the left. But where was the gunner?

Hurried footsteps sounded on the pavement. They moved to the right. Two 3-round bursts from Bolan's silenced Beretta produced no results. He eased to his feet and worked toward the Caddy. Had the gunman turned tail, or was he retreating to a better position?

Bolan fingered the two fraggers he carried on his webbing. If the target came near enough to the Cadillac, Bolan could decimate man and machine with one grenade. But that was wishful thinking.

Another booming round zapped through space, hitting a dozen feet away. Bolan's machine pistol punched out nine shots this time, aimed on both sides of the muzzle-flash. But again no hits. His target was back in the brush now, moving deeper into the woods.

The Executioner heard a clunk on the pavement and expected the worst. He dived over the two-foot log edging the parking lot as the rain-filled sky was split open by the ripping, tearing blast of a fragger. But none of the shrapnel found Bolan.

He uttered a stream of agonized screams, which became groans, then died.

The Executioner lay behind the log, the Uzi charged and ready for the man to come gloat over his kill.

11

Bolan crouched behind the log for five minutes, waiting for the Mafia hit man. He did not come. The ruse had failed. He rolled silently toward the brush, came to his feet by two sheltering trees and looked toward the parking lot.

The enemy crew wagon was still there. There was no sign of the other man but Bolan knew he was out there somewhere, a skilled, patient guerrilla fighter. The consequences of their meeting would be deadly.

The Executioner leaned around a tree and aimed the Uzi across the lot. He fired a 3-round burst into the crew wagon, then scattered six rounds where he figured the enemy might be hiding. There was no return fire.

As soon as he fired, Bolan darted to another large fir ten feet away.

Bolan pondered his next move. There was only one thing to do: flush out the gunner.

The Executioner moved through the woods silently, working away from where his enemy must be and toward the Thunderbird. There was no sign of his opponent near the car. There had been no time or opportunity for his enemy to booby-trap the vehicle.

Crouching, he ran to the rig, jumped in the passenger door and slid across to the driver's seat.

The little light inside the car had lit and darkened. Bolan watched the lot and saw a tiny light flash in the Caddy. Someone had seen and done likewise.

The Thunderbird charged across the wet pavement toward the other car. As it neared, the Caddy came to life, snarled across the lot, slithered out the exit and roared onto the highway along the Columbia River, moving eastward. The Thunderbird followed.

The highway was deserted. Bolan sent two rounds from the Beretta toward the fleeing crew wagon, and saw an answering muzzle-flash.

He tried to remember what was along the river. A few small towns. He was trying to second-guess the man in the Caddy, but his mind was drawing a blank.

The cars rocked along the freeway at sixty-five miles per hour, then accelerated to seventy-five. After a few minutes, the lead car slowed and took an off ramp toward the Oregon side of the huge Bonneville Dam, which spans the Columbia.

There was a parking lot beside the project, and a guard station, both locked.

Bolan spun the Thunderbird around to block the road to the parking lot. There was no way the crew wagon could pass.

A figure sprang from the Caddy and ran toward the gate leading into the complex. The Executioner followed with the loaded Uzi and Big Thunder ready on his hip.

Evidently there was no exterior guard at night. The man went over the first low gate, and as Bolan pursued he saw the man climb a fence that, according to a sign, led toward the fish ladders. Without hesitation, the Executioner charged after his quarry. Bolan could see no reason for the hit man to lead him here, but he did not want to lose him now.

For a moment he caught a good glimpse of his enemy under a floodlight. He was tall and looked muscular. The man vanished around a corner.

So far no one had challenged them. Probably few people trespassed there. But Bolan knew that a lot of gunfire would produce armed guards.

The man stopped near a long, inclined concrete plane with a fence on top: the fish ladders. These devices allowed salmon to leap up a series of long ladders, or steps, to spawn; the fish literally climbed upstream around the dam.

The hit man ran along the ladders to a narrow beam that crossed a twenty-foot gap. It was only twelve inches wide, and when he reached the center he spread his arms for balance.

By then Bolan was close enough to use the Beretta. The round slammed into one outstretched arm. The man fell from the narrow walkway into the concrete fish ladders six feet below. Two feet of water flowed over them.

The man tumbled down three of the wide steps, then came up brandishing a big cannon.

The weapon roared, but its round missed Bolan as he peered over the concrete side. The handgun opened up again and the round whizzed over Bolan's head. The blast reverberated in the heavy concrete-lined enclosure.

Within ten seconds lights snapped on and a spotlight moved around, searching. A voice over a loudspeaker boomed, "Put down your weapon, and surrender. You are in a restricted area of the Bonneville Power Administration. Our guards are armed and will return fire."

Bolan slipped into the shadows. He had missed his chance to snuff the hit man. Now he had to flee before the guards closed in. He retraced his steps. At the last gate, a searchlight swept over him and away, and he darted into the darkness. A voice called to him from a tower on a loudspeaker, but he ran hard for the Thunderbird.

Once inside he pulled Big Thunder from its holster and drove near the crew wagon. He rolled down the window and slammed three shots into the engine of the big car and a fourth into the gas tank. The Cadillac exploded in a fireball.

The Thunderbird roared through the exit as a Jeep with siren wailing came through a gate from the interior of the complex.

It was no contest. The Thunderbird rolled onto the highway, leaving the Jeep far behind. There was no chance the driver of the Jeep could identify the vehicle or get its license number.

AS SOON AS HE HAD TIME, Bolan wanted to contact Nino Tattaglia, a mafioso who chose to become an informant rather than spend forty years in prison. Nino could find out if the Commission had put a new bloodhound on the Executioner's trail. He could find out about this new threat:

his name, his home base, his training, his methods.

It took the Executioner almost an hour to drive to the Portland address that was his destination. He planned to tie up the loose ends of the twin-sister killings before the night was over. Untouched so far was Jody Warren, the loan shark and pimp who had put Charlotte into the situation that had provoked her death.

Warren's kingdom extended over an industrial section of Portland that once contained important ports and was now home to slums, factories, warehouses and abandoned buildings taken over by rats and derelicts.

It was after 3:00 A.M. when Bolan found the building he wanted. It was three-stories high; most of the upper windows were covered with plywood. The bottom floor, now vacant, had once been filled with a miniature farmers' market. There was probably a basement, Bolan figured.

He tried a door. The knob turned easily and the door swung open on oiled hinges. Inside a night-light glowed on a small counter. A young black man sat behind it, snoring softly, his head in his arms.

Bolan figured that since there were few blacks in the Mafia, the man was hired help, sleeping on the job. The Executioner removed a pair of plastic riot cuffs from his shoulder bag and looped and tightened one around the young man's hand before he awoke. Bolan's hand, and then a wide piece of tape went over the struggling youth's mouth. Another cuff went around an ankle, and Bolan put him behind the counter on the floor.

In the first room on the ground floor was a torture chamber, containing whips, ropes, high-watt floodlights, chairs nailed to the floor, a motorcycle chain and numerous brass knuckles. Bolan took two steps into the room and the floor gave way beneath him.

With a desperate lunge he made it back to safety and watched as a trapdoor swung down, revealing a pit below. The bottom was filled with Nam-type sharpened punji stakes pointing upward.

He went along a hall to another room. Soft noises came from behind the door. It was locked. He quickly picked the lock and swung the door open. In the dim light he saw six wooden cages made of two-by-fours, each four feet square and each containing a naked girl. Four were white, two black. All but one was asleep. She curled up and glared at him.

"No, not again!" she cried. "I'll do it! I'll do anything now!"

He tested the floor, then stepped to the cages and wrenched the wooden and wire doors off their hinges. He told the captives to find their clothes and get away if they could.

The next room could have been a drug-cutting room. There was no trace of illegal substances in the room, but on a long table was a set of sensitive scales.

Hearing something behind him, he turned as a large black man hurtled toward him. Bolan sidestepped the diving man and drove his knee upward into his side. The man hit the floor, rolled and returned to his feet, arms held wide like a wrestler's. He started to reach for a revolver at his belt, but Bolan's 93-R came up first and chugged once, drilling a small neat hole through the attacker's heart, dropping him to the wooden floor.

Bolan spun as the door opened. A tall black girl entered, wearing only a short see-through nightie. She saw the girls getting out of the cages and smiled.

"Hey, honkie, if you really want to help us, come this way. That white trash lives on the third floor, and almost nobody gets up there to see him after he sets the switches. Come take a look."

She was about five-ten, with a centerfold body, and seemed totally at ease. She motioned, and he followed her out of the room and along the hall to a door at the end. It opened into a room in which a circular stairway wound upward.

The black girl led the way. At the second story Bolan saw the thick metal plate that, when in position, sealed the upper floors from below, and saw how it could be reinforced with two-inch bars of steel. Fortunately the metal door was open; unfortunately there was no ladder continuing to the top floor.

The black girl stepped off the stairway and pointed down a dimly lit hall. "He calls it the Hallway of Terrors. See how shiny that part of the hall floor is? It's usually electrically charged with enough juice to kill the giant rats that run round this place."

"What's in the rooms?"

"I don't know. I've never been farther than this. In one of them is another circular staircase to the bastard's private lair. He's got one or two ladies up there who we never see. He gets his supplies from a small dumbwaiter, too small for any of us to get inside."

They entered a room containing a cot, a dresser and two wooden chairs.

"A good short on that electrical field should blow out all the power in the place," Bolan said.

The black girl shook her head. "He built it with that in mind, at first for the rats. Then he surged the power and put in a whole box of circuit breakers and automatic resets. The controls are in that room." She pointed to the opposite end of the hall.

Bolan picked up a wooden chair and threw it onto the electrified part of the floor.

Blue flames shot outward. The chair's legs smoldered where they touched the floor. Then the zapping electrical fire died.

The Executioner counted how long it took for the circuit-breaker resets to activate the power again.

After twenty seconds the power returned, sending smoking, crackling, blue flames along the hall. After thirty seconds it went off again. As soon as the smoking stopped he charged across the electrified part of the floor, kicked open the door to the control room, then raced inside and turned off the electrical skillet just before the power was due to return.

The room was about ten feet square, with a second door, open two inches, on the opposite wall. Bolan stepped into the small sunken space where the door swung open, the only unused space in the room. The rest was filled with snakes, enclosed by a three-foot Plexiglas wall that was concave to prevent their escape.

A nest of diamondback rattlesnakes owned one part of the floor, which had been covered with sand, rocks and soil. A pair of king cobras were coiled near the center. A few sections of logs were scattered around. All anyone had to do to get across the room was jump over the wall, travel ten feet through the snake den, and jump over the other three-foot barrier to the far door.

Bolan watched. Dozens of small snakes writhed on the sand, matching the color so well they were easy to miss. About fifty black two-foot snakes slithered throughout the enclosure. Bolan figured every snake in the pit was poisonous.

Where did the other doors in the hall lead? He looked down the hall as the power returned and the chair again smoldered. One door had been nailed to its frame—the bright silver heads of twenty penny-nails showed.

The black girl stood at the edge of the electrified floor. Bolan asked, "You have any hair spray?"

"Sure. Two new cans. Why?"

"Get both for me as fast as you can."

She vanished. Bolan turned back to the snakes. He could see no pattern in their movement, no safe route through their midst. He would have to risk it. There was one element that all wild animals feared and gave way to. He hoped that the snakes obeyed this univer-sal law of nature.

The black girl returned.

"I found three," she said. She tossed them one at a time across the electrified floor, and he caught them, put one in each side pocket, took the last and hit the pressure button. A fine chemical spray jetted out. Good, lots of pressure.

He used his cigarette lighter to ignite the hair spray. A second later he had a small blowtorch, blasting a column of fire a foot long. He leaned over the plastic barrier and aimed the fire at a nest of small black snakes, and they slithered away. The sand-colored ones were next, and they retreated also, leaving two square feet free of snakes.

When the area was cleared as far as he could reach, Bolan jumped over the wall and swept the torch from side to side in a two-foot arc as he moved across the room.

Halfway across the flame sputtered. He lit the second can and continued. When he saw the slowly weaving head in front of him he stopped. One of the king cobras did not retreat from the fire. Bolan let it sense the heat. He thrust the flame upward and singed its eyes and skin, and it moved away.

Behind him, the snakes were closing in almost as fast as he moved forward. A big diamondback rattlesnake slithered forward, curiously watched his boots, then coiled and rattled. That brought a dozen more rattles as other snakes sensed the danger. Bolan sensed danger, too, but continued, even as the second cobra approached him. The flame flickered, and he removed the third can from his pocket. It refused to light. He tossed it at the deadly snake. In the split second that its head darted sideways to hit the can, Bolan's boot caught the cobra on the side of the head. The force of his kick lifted it off the floor and flung it to the far wall.

In the same movement The Executioner reached the far wall and vaulted out of the pit. He wiped the sweat off his forehead and glanced back. His path was again covered by the killer snakes.

He turned and looked into the next chamber in this house of horrors. His face twisted in surprise, and he cursed at the trial awaiting him.

12

Through the center of the twelve-foot-square room ran a double barbed-wire fence. On the fence hung two red triangular signs with white lettering: MINE FIELD.

The floor was covered by two feet of sand, gravel, a few small rocks and some rotted sagebrush. The dirt had been laid out with a small hill in the middle, sloping down toward the door. There were a hundred places to put land mines. Were they really there, or was it a bluff?

The ceiling had originally been painted white but now showed evidence of an explosion: the center had been sprayed with shrapnel and the black smoke of a blast.

A piece of yellow paper had been taped to the low circular retaining wall around the sand, which cleared an area so that the door could open. Bolan stooped to read the writing on it:

Welcome to Desert Acres. Your short walk through this mine field should be eventful. More than forty different mines are planted here, and some where nobody would expect them. Most are normal U.S. Army antipersonnel mines,

which are easy to dig in and easy to set off with
the merest touch. A few highly interesting mine-
bombs are planted here as well. These are home-
made, and at least one is a "positional" type
device. It is currently exactly level. If it is tilted,
it will blast you straight to hell.

Incidentally, the ceiling and walls of this room
are specially constructed with ship plate steel.

Good luck on your little journey. It should be
a most memorable one. A last tip. Don't attempt
to walk around the walls. The last person who
tried got one hell of a surprise—and is no longer
with us!

Bolan examined the sand. He knew most of the
Army mines forward and backward.

One look at the snakes behind him made him de-
cide. Without a blowtorch he could not return
through the snakes. He had to proceed.

He checked for snakes in the sand. There were
none. Then he leaned over the retaining wall and
examined the surface of the "desert." He saw a
slender wire-loop trigger extending a quarter inch
from the sand. Carefully he studied the position from
which this mine could be dug out. It was an old trick,
to string several mines together. When the digger
started removing one, he set off another, and the
party was over.

Bolan found three mines interlocked in a tight row.
Working on them one by one, still leaning over the
wall, he removed the sand meticulously. When he
was sure no others were attached, he worked faster

and removed the first mine, then the second and at last the third. He left the dirt disturbed so he could tell where to walk.

As he stepped over the wall into the sand, he wished he could blast a path to the far door with the Uzi, but in the confined space one blast would set off another, and he'd have no protection from the shrapnel.

His fingers moved cautiously over the sand, not in a straight line to the far door, but in a lateral direction, around the side of the small hill. The shortest route would be the most heavily implanted.

Bolan found no mine for a two-foot span, so he carefully scraped a line across the span three inches deep. He found a trigger barely two inches under the surface, a foot from the last mine.

Sweating, he slung the Uzi over his back to get it out of the way, then removed the mine and put it to the far side, where he would not kick it or place it near a sensitive mine trigger.

Ten minutes later he had removed four more mines and was halfway across the room.

He remembered that the note said something about mines being where no one would expect. What did that mean? The Executioner looked at the retaining wall by the other door and decided he had to clear another three feet, step to the wall and jump to the floor.

No!

There would be a mine planted under the floor, he realized. Make it all the way across and then blow yourself up when you thought you were home safe.

He knelt in the safe sand and stared ahead. He had angled his approach toward the end of the retaining wall beside the door, which was open slightly and swung inward.

One more mine came free. It was a different type, and Bolan hoped it could be laid on its side. He held his breath as he put it down, then exhaled.

His fingers found yet another type of device an inch under the surface. It was ten to twelve inches, square. He detoured around it.

Bolan moved one more routine antipersonnel mine and stood. His foot could touch the wall. But the more he studied this side of the wall the more he realized it was different from the other side. Four inches from the wall a loop trip wire extended from the retaining boards.

Bolan removed another mine so he could step closer to the door, then leaned over and swung the door inward so he could examine it and the wooden floor. Two mines lay there, with boards resting on the triggers. Touching either board would be deadly.

He looked into the room beyond and saw a regular floor that once had been covered with linoleum tile. Now some had loosened and come off.

Leaning, he caught the top of the door and rode with it as it closed, swinging over the last two mines and touching down in the next room as his hands were about to hit the doorjamb.

The Executioner glanced at his watch. It was after 4:00 A.M. Plenty of time.

He did not need any more surprises. What was unusual and deadly about this room? There had to be

something. Jody Warren was not going to give anyone a free pass through it. Did the missing nine-inch
squares of tile form a pattern? No, they were random. He studied the floor. Why were some tiles
removed? They had not been curled or steamed off.
He examined the nearest bare spot. Strips of black
adhesive that had once held the tile were still visible.
Around the spot the floor had been gouged and
scraped.

The tiles had been removed on purpose.

Why?

Bolan turned and delicately lifted the half-inch
board from the mine trigger. It was four feet long.
He pushed an edge of the board against the floor
where the tile had been. Nothing happened. He
swung it ahead and jammed it down on the next
empty square.

There was an immediate "spanging" sound, and a
dartlike arrow whizzed across the room and embed-
ded itself in the far wall.

The Executioner studied the near wall and saw a
small slit four feet high. The wall was evidently an
addition, built to conceal something. He could see
slots along this false wall, some four feet, a few three
feet high.

He watched the wall as he pushed the board
against another bare square. A black dart flashed
from a slot and rammed into the far wall.

Crouching, Bolan moved toward the far wall, carefully avoiding the squares with no tiles. Finally he
reached the door. When he tried the handle, it would
not budge. Locked.

The time for finesse was over. Bolan still sweated from the nerve-jangling bout with the mines. He stepped back and drove his right foot forward, mightily kicking the door below the doorknob. It sprang open.

The room ahead was smaller, and empty except for another iron spiral staircase at the far end. He detected no booby traps. He held the Uzi as he walked toward the staircase. Nothing moved.

No sounds came.

He looked up the staircase and found the same type of dim electric lights that existed in all the rooms. With a critical eye, he cased the small room. No hidden dangers were apparent. Maybe he was through the gauntlet.

Electrified stairs? Easy enough, since they were metal. He dropped a penny on the metal. Nothing unusual happened. He touched then gripped the hand rail.

He moved up the steps soundlessly, the Uzi raised, his finger on the trigger. There was no steel plate barring the top of the stairs. At last he had access to the inner sanctum of Jody Warren, Beast of Portland.

He climbed to a small landing, and peered into it over the top of the ladder. Sensing no danger, he continued upward into the room. It was about eight feet square, bare except for a door.

Soft music sounded from concealed speakers. Bolan tested the door. Unlocked. He opened it slightly and peeked into the next room. He saw an old-fashioned parlor with a couch, chairs, a spindle-legged dining-room table in heavy oak and four oak straight-backed chairs with cane-laced seats.

Antique tintypes and a large, oval, glass-framed picture of a dour man and woman decorated the walls. The man had a heavy mustache and stood behind the chair in which the woman sat, looking very prim and proper.

Bolan hurried across the room to another door. Beyond was a kitchen and a bath, and farther on, a large bedroom. A man and two women, all naked, lay sleeping on the king-size bed.

JODY WARREN WAS SHORT AND FAT. His stringy brown hair was scattered over the pillow. Acne scars pocked his face. Brownish stains, possibly from lack of washing, splotched his face and neck. He mumbled in his sleep and reached for the closest girl.

The Executioner held the Uzi an inch above his ear and fired into the wall. Warren jolted upward, his eyes wild. He saw Bolan in the soft night-lights and swore. Both women jumped up, screaming. Warren yelled, "Who are you? And who the hell let you in?"

Bolan tossed a marksman's medal onto the bed and the small man began to shake.

"Hey, it ain't me you want. Get the big shots. Me, I'm small potatoes. Get the bosses!"

"They come next, Jody."

At a sign from Bolan, the women moved off the bed and out of danger.

"Get your pants on, Jody. I hate to see a man die when he's naked."

"Hey, you got no fight with me. I just follow

orders." He started to rise from the bed, rolled over and grabbed a .45 automatic from under the big pillow. Bolan slammed three shots through his wrist, and flesh and blood and bone sprayed as the heavy gun fell to the sheets.

"Bastard!"

"Get your pants on."

With his good hand, Jody picked up a pair of blue pants from a chair and got into them. He was in agony.

"May I bandage his hand?" one of the women asked. Bolan nodded. The tall slender brunette took a scarf from a dresser and wound it around the wrist, stopping the bleeding.

"Now show me how you turn off the juice in that hallway, Jody."

Jody glared at him in fury, then motioned with his bandaged hand. "Down here."

The Executioner followed him through another room to a closet. Warren leaped on a brass pole and slid through the floor.

A fireman's pole!

The Executioner grabbed the pole and dropped into the blackness below. There was no light, absolutely none at all. Bolan guessed he had landed in a second-floor room on the far side of the hallway. He held his breath. Hearing a movement to the left, he drew the silenced Beretta and fired three single shots.

Then the Executioner snapped on his cigarette lighter. The small flame revealed a figure cowering in the corner.

"Nice try, but you're still a dead man, Jody. Now how do you turn off the juice?"

"It's on a timer."

"Where is the door in here?"

Jody pointed to the right in the flickering light.

"Open it."

Warren rose and opened the door. He looked into the hall. The slick, electrified surface seemed unchanged, except that now a charred wooden chair lay on the floor.

"Juice is off," Bolan said. "It must have burned out your reset."

Then Warren dashed into the hall, ran past two doorways and through a third.

Bolan caught the slamming door and stopped six steps behind Warren, realizing they were in the mechanical dart room with the patchwork linoleum floor.

Bolan watched the pimp and loan shark hopscotch across the floor, and followed exactly in his footsteps. Then his quarry burst into the mined room, tripped over the retaining wall and fell into the sand. He turned to Bolan with fear on his face.

Bolan stopped at the door, the Uzi up, amazement on his face. "How the hell did you miss the mines?"

"I didn't. There's only one in here that's live. The rest are practice mines with no charges."

"Let's find the live one," Bolan said, triggering the Uzi into the sand, hoping one of the slugs would detonate the mine.

"No! That's not fair!"

"Tell Charlotte Albers about fair, you bastard."

Shielded by the door, Bolan moved his fire to the other side of the room.

One slug found the right spot and the room exploded with a deafening roar that slammed the Executioner back into the dart room. He felt a sting on the arm that had been exposed, and saw a four-inch gash where shrapnel had penetrated. A red stream poured out.

He returned to the door. The mangled, bloody remains of Jody Warren were strewn near the far door.

"That one was for Charlotte and Charleen," Bolan said.

The electricity was still off in the hall. Bolan hurried across it to the end room, and found the black girl dressed in street clothes, waiting for him.

"Glad you won," she said. "I got everybody else out. Just the girls in trouble were here. I told them never to come back. I don't care about the bitches upstairs. We better split, cause the cops gonna be here in a couple of minutes."

Bolan nodded. He let the Uzi hang on its cord, and they paced out to the street.

The black girl looked at him.

"Don't know who you are, but thanks for the vermin extermination." She paused. "Hey, if you ever..." She stopped and shook her head. "No way, girl. This man don't ever have to pay for his loving." She grinned. "Been nice," she said. "Thanks again." She walked away into the Portland dawn.

As the Executioner got into his Thunderbird, the rain began again, soft and cleansing.

13

It was after 5:00 A.M. when Mack Bolan unlocked his hotel door and entered the room. He sensed someone there and crouched, then snapped on the light.

Johnny slept on the bed, fully clothed. He sat up, rubbed his eyes and grinned.

"Guess I dropped off to sleep."

"Yeah." Bolan went to his suitcase, took out a first-aid kit and broke it open. Johnny was beside him in a minute, checking the slashed left arm, taking over. He cleaned it with a wet washcloth, doused it with antiseptic, put a compress over it and bandaged it tightly.

Mack Bolan inspected his wound, then put on a clean black jersey and looked at Johnny. "When is that ship due to dock?"

"At 1330 hours, one-thirty, at Terminal One, berth fifteen."

"So it'll enter the mouth of the Columbia about daylight. I should be able to find it along the Columbia on the way."

"You need help?"

"I need two hours sleep. Then I'll be ready to go. See if any of the helicopter rental agencies are open yet. See if you can find one that has a pilot who flew choppers in Nam, and find out about renting a bird from eight o'clock to about noon, cash in advance.''

Johnny nodded and turned to the phone book. Before he found what he was looking for, the Executioner was asleep.

AT NINE A.M. BOLAN AND SCOOTER ROICK slanted down the Willamette River from the Portland International Airport. Both were scanning the water. They were flying a Bell Jet Ranger, with enough speed and power for the job.

Scooter Roick was a lean man of about thirty-five. His eyes danced when Bolan told him that what they were about to do was highly illegal but that Scooter would be only marginally involved.

"Damn, just like Nam. Most of what we did there was a little wild, too!"

"Some guys on deck may shoot at us with handguns or rifles," the Executioner said. "Are you still game?"

"Hell, yes! I haven't had any fun in years. You want me to set you down on the fantail of some freighter?"

"Right. She'll be moving upstream at maybe ten knots. Get me within eight or ten feet of the deck, and I'll go down a rope. There might be some guy wires or cranes on this thing. I don't know.''

"Man, I'll put you down so you can step off.''

"This freighter is smuggling a load of arms and ammunition to the Mafia for terrorist training. It's my job to stop the shipment from getting to port.''

They talked about Nam for a while as they flew

along the Willamette to the mouth of the mighty Columbia River as it flowed toward Astoria and the Pacific Ocean. They spotted a freighter coming upstream, but it showed a Dutch flag and was riding high in the water.

They continued downstream. Ten minutes later they saw another freighter.

"Japanese flag," Bolan said. They came down for a closer look. The name on the bow was *Karatsu Maru*. "That's our baby, Scooter. How does she look?"

"Piece of cake. There's that short mast right on the stern, but there aren't any cranes or lines stretched around. I can get you within three feet of the deck."

Bolan nodded. "We go on downstream until we're out of sight, then turn and come back at them low over the water."

"You got it!"

They continued downstream, made a sweeping turn over green woods and fields, and returned at reduced speed, barely above the river.

Bolan checked the Uzi, hung around his neck. His combat harness was filled with the usual gear and two smoke grenades. Big Thunder clung to his thigh and the Beretta 93-R nestled in shoulder leather.

"Let's do it!" Bolan said.

The chopper raced up-current, came around a bend and found the black stern and churning wake of the Japanese freighter three hundred yards ahead. Bolan looked down and saw water no more than two feet below. He hoped they did not hit a sudden downdraft.

He checked the latch on the outward swinging door.

Scooter looked over and grinned. "In another thirty seconds I'll lift our nose up and come over that fantail, then drop down, almost touching the left-hand side of the deck. You ready?"

Bolan unbuckled his seat belt.

Scooter momentarily scrutinized the controls, then the water and the black hulk ahead. "Now!" he yelled. The craft lifted like an elevator and nosed over the thirty-foot wall of steel. Bolan slammed back the door and jumped. An instant later he rolled onto the deck of the *Karatsu Maru*.

He ran behind a small shack near the center of the big deck. At once the chopper lifted and headed downstream at full throttle. Bolan had seen no guards or seamen. No shots had been fired.

Two men rushed past Bolan to the stern rail and watched the chopper disappear. One was obviously a Mafia soldier. He held an old model .45 automatic. The other was a Japanese seaman wearing blue jeans and a blue T-shirt.

"Now what the hell was that all about?" the hood said.

"Friendly American hello?" the puzzled Japanese said in heavily accented English.

The soldier shook his head. "I think we got trouble."

"Yeah, back here," Bolan said, the 93-R in his right hand.

The hood spun, his .45 ready before he had seen a target.

Bolan fired. The shot took the hood under the chin and traveled upward through his brain. The Executioner rushed to the rail and flipped the Mafia corpse over the barrier into the churning wake.

Bolan turned to the stunned Oriental. "Friend," Bolan said, looking at the seaman. "I won't hurt you. How many bad Americans like him are on board?"

The Japanese sailor's eyes were still wide. "You...you...killed him!"

"Yes. He's a Mafia criminal. How many?"

"Four. They come with river pilot at Astoria."

The Executioner scowled. It figured Canzonari would want some protection coming upstream. He motioned for the Japanese to follow him, and they squatted behind the metal shack for cover.

"Do the other Mafia guys have guns?"

"Yes, big pistols. Most of them two guns."

"Have they hurt any of your crew?"

"No, but Captain most unhappy."

"I bet he is. Can you bring one of the Americans back here?"

"Not if you kill him."

"Yes. I understand. Where are they?"

"One with pilot, one in captain's cabin with captain. Other two...." The Japanese shrugged.

"Do you know there are illegal guns on board, thousands of them?"

"No, industrial machinery!"

"Big closed boxes?"

"Yes."

Bolan asked the seaman to direct him to the captain's cabin. Then he ran past three cargo hatches to the superstructure. There were three decks above. He slipped through a doorway and climbed some steps to the top deck and found the room he had been told was the captain's cabin.

The Executioner tested the doorknob. It moved. He turned it as far as it would go to the right, held the 93-R in his left hand and quietly and quickly opened the door.

It was a big cabin with a window. A Japanese man—the captain, Bolan guessed—sat in a soft chair. A tall Mafia soldier wearing jeans and a T-shirt and a black stocking cap stood looking out to sea.

"I thought I saw a white man down there," muttered the hardman. "You got anybody else on board?" He glared at the captain, a heavy handgun held at his side.

"I'm right here, bad-ass," Bolan said quietly. The soldier spun, his piece coming up, but it never reached target. A 9mm slug punched a widening hole through the side of the soldier's head, killing him with only the sound of a gentle cough.

The captain leaped to his feet, chattering in Japanese. At that moment the seaman Bolan had met below entered and began translating.

"Captain Ohura wants to know if you are one of the criminals."

"No. I'm here to help him, to help all of you and to stop the hidden arms from reaching their new owners."

The crewman translated. The bilingual man listened to the captain speak, then turned to Bolan. "Then you are a policeman. Welcome. Now we must retake the bridge. Another pirate is there with the river pilot, and you may kill the criminal, also, if you wish."

Bolan grinned. "You lead," he said. The seaman spoke briefly to the captain, who took a small automatic from a handsome mahogany cabinet. Then they left the cabin and moved forward and to the left, as the seaman indicated.

"That's the door. Inside are three big windows, and navigational and operating instruments. The pilot knows the river and he steers us upstream to the port."

The captain spoke quietly but sharply. The seaman listened, then translated. "Captain Ohura says he must fight this battle. It is his honor. I am to enter the room first to distract the Mafia man. My captain will capture him."

"Tell him I'll back him up at the door."

Bolan stood by the wall beside the door and watched the seaman open it and enter the room.

"What the hell! Told you guys to stay off the bridge!" The voice was a roar.

The seaman muttered something softly.

"What the hell! Speak up!"

The captain bolted into the room. Bolan followed, aware that more than one Mafia soldier might be inside.

There was not.

The captain yelled something in Japanese in a wild, high voice, then shot the Mafia soldier. The report on the handgun sounded like a .32 to Bolan, who watched the hoodlum take four rounds in the chest, then drop the .45 automatic he carried and collapse. There was no need to check his condition.

The American pilot at the electronic steering board stared in amazement.

"What's going on here? First these gunmen take over the ship, and now the captain shoots this guy down in a rage. And who are you?"

"You just got a gun out of your ribs, joker. Don't push your luck. You do your job, we'll do ours."

The Japanese were talking quietly. The bilingual seaman approached Bolan. "My captain says he will stay here with door locked. I show you where last two are. He says you may kill them."

"Let's go find the other two rats in your holds."

They descended metal ladders, traveled along the deck, then down more ladders into a dark hold. It was jammed with big boxes and pallets of goods stacked high against the walls. Ahead, by a bright light, two men were laughing and joking as they wiped grease off a pair of submachine guns. A large cargo box was open beside them. Bolan noticed that neither seemed to be familiar with the big weapons, and neither held side arms.

Bolan lifted the Uzi, made sure it was charged with a round and crept forward in the gloom. He stopped beside two heavy pine boxes and looked around. The men were trying to load a magazine with rounds. The two weapons were German-made MP-40 submachine guns.

"You've got to release the operating lever first,

guys," Bolan said from twenty feet away. Both men dropped the machine guns and dug for hand weapons.

The Executioner triggered a 5-round burst at the faster one, dumping him on the floor in front of the box with four holes in his chest. The slower one dived to the floor and crawled behind a wooden box. Bolan motioned for the seaman to stay put and ran ahead to the cover of an eight-foot-square box, the first in a row.

There was no sound. Stepping on a small crate, Bolan boosted himself on top of the tall box. He bellied across it and looked down an aisle. Nothing. He jumped to the next box, and bellied across it and looked down. More nothing. He jumped to a third box and looked down. The gunman lay directly below, his .45 two feet from his hand.

Bolan stood.

The gunman lunged for his weapon.

"Touch it and you're full of lead." The hand stopped moving. "Some questions. You work for Canzonari?"

"Yes."

"Will he be at dockside at one-thirty today?"

"Yes, him and Joey."

"Good. Now stand up and walk back to those MP-40s. Put them away so all looks fine. Are all of the hidden weapons in this hold?"

"Yes. I saw the loading manifest."

"Move it."

The soldier repacked the two submachine guns in the box, replaced the box in the larger crate and nailed it shut. It took five minutes.

The box looked enough like the other crates now to pass. Bolan was about to order the mobster to move, when he heard someone coming.

Captain Ohura stepped into the glow of the bare bulb in the cargo hold, and glared at the hoodlum without speaking.

Then the Japanese skipper took out his small automatic and shot the hood in the head three times at point-blank range.

14

The Executioner watched as the Japanese maritime captain fired twice more into the Mafia gunman after he fell to the floor. The captain intoned something in an urgent voice and marched away.

Bolan turned to the interpreter.

"The captain says this man has no right to live, no right to dirty the captain's good name by using his ship for smuggling."

"I have some suggestions," Bolan said. "First you hide the dead Mafia gunmen in a locker. Then I want to see who comes to pick up the guns. When your captain calms down, explain this to him. There will be no problems for him over the smuggled guns."

The Japanese seaman nodded grimly. "I try, but captain is furious. We have three hours before docking. I better go free rest of crew."

Bolan went topside and talked with the pilot.

"Three hours is all I need," Bolan instructed. "Do not mention the Mafia hoodlums or the killings to the customs and immigration inspector. At the end of that time you can tell the port authorities, the FBI and the Portland Police Department anything you want."

The pilot was in his midforties and had been up and down the river between Portland and The Dalles more times than he could count.

"This is the craziest ride I've ever had. Those guys really Mafia hoodlums?"

"They're all dead. The captain took care of the last two himself."

The pilot was thoughtful for a moment.

"Say I go along with this. What do I tell them when they find out I clammed up for three hours? They'll lift my ticket. I'll be out of a job."

"No way. Show them this." Bolan handed him a marksman's badge. "Tell them I threatened you and your family."

The pilot grinned as he steered the big ship through a narrow opening in the channel and continued up the Willamette toward Portland.

"Man, you got it all figured out."

"Now if I can convince Captain Ohura. He's the tough one."

Bolan found the captain in his cabin and talked to him for an hour; talked until the interpreter's mouth was dry. He used every argument he could. At last the captain laughed.

"Because you and I, we resisted those pirates, killed all five, I will do it. I will wait three hours before launching my protest about pirates. And I know nothing of smuggled arms."

BOLAN CHECKED HIS GEAR. He still had everything he needed. He returned to the hold where the illegal weapons were stashed and checked the destination labels. The boxes were going to Johnson Farm Equipment Corporation in Gresham.

Back on deck, Bolan saw the towns become larger as the vessel approached the outskirts of Portland. Now all he had to do was find a safe hiding place until the customs men finished their work.

He hoped the freighter captain had a fast turnaround so the cargo would be off-loaded at once. Longshoremen would tie up the big ship, then the customs inspector would check the goods against the manifest and give them authority to unload. That could take an hour or two. It would be a simple offload. There were fifteen large wooden crates. They would probably be hoisted from the hold right onto trucks on the dock.

He hid in the most obvious place, the captain's cabin. He had taken off his combat harness and all his weapons and packed them in a gunnysack he found in one of the holds.

The ship docked on schedule and everything followed the usual routine. Immigration approved all of the merchant seamen's papers; a customs official went into the hold and inspected the big boxes, counted them and gave the signal to unload. The hatch covers came off and big gantry cranes lifted the boxes from the hold and lowered them onto flatbed trailers behind highway diesel tractors that ground away from the dock.

The immigration man spoke briefly with the captain, then left. The customs agent sat in a camper on the dock, counting the big boxes as they came down. He had his cooler open, and hoisted a cold beer as he listened to an afternoon baseball game on a radio.

Bolan waved at the captain as he walked down the short gangway to the dock. No one stopped him. He saw that the last of the boxes were coming down. There were too many for the trucks. Some of the rigs would have to make two trips.

The Executioner knew the address, but there was a chance they might not go to that location. He phoned a local rental-car agency. Yes, they could deliver a rental car to him at the Port of Portland Terminal One. The driver would be there in fifteen minutes.

GRESHAM IS EAST OF PORTLAND, toward the mountains. Bolan drove the two-year-old Mercury west of the town to a big sign that read: JOHNSON FARM EQUIPMENT. Several tractors, combines, mowers and plows were parked at one end of the big lot. The Executioner drove past and parked at the far side.

In the rearview mirror he saw a big truck with large wooden boxes on its flatbed enter the main gate and circle behind a long warehouse. This would be a daylight operation.

Bolan shrugged into his combat webbing, put four fraggers on the straps and set the Big Thunder holster on his belt. The 93-R dropped into shoulder leather, and he was ready. He drove down one block, took a right and found a road behind the farm-equipment dealership.

About a block down the road were a half-dozen fir trees that had never been cleared. The Executioner parked his green Mercury under them and looked at the back of the dealership.

The warehouse had no rear windows, and no activity was apparent at either end. He walked through the tall grass of the vacant field, hopped a four-foot chain-link fence and dodged behind a large combine that was too far gone to repair. It looked as though it had been cannibalized for parts.

There was not much activity in that section of the back lot. Bolan watched the warehouse door. After a few minutes a big diesel engine strained as it pulled around the back, and a truck-sized door in the warehouse, the one nearest him, rolled upward. The vehicle backed in and several laborers began unloading the heavy boxes with an overhead crane.

Other trucks arrived with three boxes on each. The last truck brought only two; the driver said, "That's the last of it." He pulled away and the large door rolled down. A man-size door opened and six laborers came out. Ten minutes later four crew wagons rolled into the yard and eight men emerged from each one. Bolan knew who they were. They were the "visitors," top weapons men from each of the families on the West Coast, there to pick up their consignment of weapons.

Greed and a hunger for murder had brought these men here. Their eyes would be glazed with a fever for the guns. The hollow men from the Mob would be careless of anything else that went on in the industrial wasteland of which the Johnson Farm Equipment site was a part. To them, the only things truly visible were the two facts uppermost in their minds: get the deal over with; and get it over with fast.

Three minutes after they filed through the door, Bolan stepped from behind the combine and walked to the door as if he belonged there. No one challenged him. He entered swiftly, took in the setup at a glance, and disappeared behind an assortment of farm machinery that had evidently been displaced by the weapons shipment.

The men who had just arrived were clustered around one of the wooden crates. Its sides had been ripped off, revealing parts of farm machinery, and also cases of arms and ammunition, rockets, rifles and MP-40 submachine guns. A light shone above them.

Bolan moved through the semidarkness to get closer to the assembly.

A voice rose above the general hubbub. "He told us not to open any of the boxes until he got here!"

"So what? He ain't *capo*. So we open a few. What's to hurt?"

Boards were pried away with crowbars, and one Mafia hit man held up an MP-40.

"Wow! What I woulda given to have this baby last night!"

A dozen of the Mafia hoodlums echoed his wish.

Bolan knew he couldn't wait for Joey Canzonari. He moved closer, lifted the four grenades from his webbing and picked his targets.

He threw the explosives, two on the side where most of the men stood, one in the middle, a fourth on the far side. The first two exploded with a shattering roar. Men screamed. Small arms fire sounded. The last pair of fraggers caught the men rushing away from the first explosions. In all, more than half the men were goners, and many of the rest screeched in pain and agony.

The Executioner settled behind a bulldozer and fired over it. Every man who held a gun became a target. Nobody knew where the silenced shots came from. Six men hid behind the big box. Bolan picked off three of them with two bursts from the silenced Beretta.

"I'm getting the hell outa here!" a voice screamed.

"Yeah? Where you going, dumb ass? Get on the floor and find out who's shooting."

A man rose and ran for the far door. Bolan brought him down with two slugs of a 3-round burst.

More random firing sounded. Then a commanding voice rang out, "Cease fire, dammit! Don't shoot unless you got a good target. Look for the bastard!"

Bolan spotted the man who had spoken.

The man continued, "Hold your fire until we get a fix on the—"

His final words were cut off as one carefully aimed round jolted through his forehead, spilling his brains.

Bolan worked quietly toward the door. The explosions might bring the police, or might not, this place being some distance out of town.

He took a smoke bomb from his webbing and pulled the pin. He threw it as far as he could into the warehouse. It went off with a pop, and heavy, thick smoke rolled out.

"Fire!" somebody screamed.

Bolan found the way to the door was blocked by a heavyset Mafia soldier looking the other way and waving a .45. He turned when Bolan coughed, and swung his gun around. The Beretta sneezed twice and the hulk died where he stood, his finger too slack to pull the trigger.

The Executioner jumped for the door, exited and darted behind the big combine outside.

A sleek black Cadillac wheeled up, and its driver jumped out and ran for the warehouse, his weapon ready. A younger man stepped from the back seat, noticing the smoke pouring from the structure.

"Joey?" Bolan called.

The young man spun around, stared at the combine. The Executioner revealed himself, and Joey Canzonari jumped behind the wheel of his Caddy and skidded away.

Bolan ran toward one of the four crew wagons. The keys were still in it, as per Mafia practice whenever a fast getaway is anticipated. He leaped in, started it, and gunned after the gangster. Joey was a quarter of a mile ahead, speeding through a red light.

Bolan was not sure where the guy was going, but he chased loyally. They turned onto the broad highway to Sandy. The only place to go from there was south over secondary roads toward Salem or around the Mount Hood Loop highway.

The cars slashed through the early-afternoon traffic at seventy-five miles an hour. Then the road narrowed and signs promised Alder Creek and Brightwood. They were on the quiet Mount Hood tourist highway. Bolan wondered when and where the Mafia Don's son would stop and fight.

15

The two vehicles wound upward into the Mount Hood National Forest. Bolan decided to put the other car off the road for a final confrontation. He raced alongside and nudged the other rig, hearing sheet metal scrape. But the other Cadillac was as heavy as his and could not be budged. Joey raised a pistol, but before he fired, Bolan hit the brakes and eased back.

Next he crept up on the bumper of the Caddy, nosed against it and tromped on the gas. The car shot ahead faster. Bolan pulled back from the swerving rig and took out Big Thunder. It was time for a sure thing.

He aimed at the left rear tire, waited for a straight stretch of road and fired. The heavy slug blew a four-inch gash in the tire.

Joey's Cadillac swerved to the left, bolted across the oncoming traffic lanes, nosed through a ditch, climbed six feet up a stand of Douglas firs and rolled over into the ditch.

The Executioner parked on the shoulder and ran toward the overturned car. Twenty feet away, he stopped and readied the Beretta 93-R.

Water hissed from the crumpled radiator. Bolan

approached the rig and looked in the upside-down rear window. He could not see a body inside. He looked on the passenger's side.

No one there.

A twig snapped in the brush above him. Bolan jerked up and saw the flash of a yellow shirt as someone darted into the undergrowth.

The jungle fighter dropped to the ground, crawled through the fern and light brush to a two-foot-thick fir and stood behind it. Now he was in his element. Now he was in Vietnam.

Faint footsteps sounded ahead. The Executioner lifted the Beretta and advanced to the next thick tree. Again he held his breath and listened.

The footsteps were clearer now and came from straight ahead. Bolan tried to visualize the map. They had not yet come to the little town of Rhododendron, so they were several miles west of the peak of Mount Hood, which rose to over eleven thousand feet and carried a snowcap year round. But they were high enough on the slopes that there were ten miles of untracked wilderness ahead of them. Going north the way Joey was heading, they could hike all the way to the Columbia River highway before they found a road. The guy must be planning to circle back.

Twice more Bolan charged ahead, following a faint trail of crushed ferns and the sounds of flight. Then he saw Canzonari cross a small clearing. The Mafia specialist turned, snapped off a quick shot and disappeared into the woods.

His young prey was moving slower now, the Executioner could tell. He was a city boy, getting tired. Whereas the trail had been through the thick brush of the rain forest, now it met a game trail where deer moved for water and forage. Bolan was sure that Joey would use the trail as the path of least resistance.

He charged along a small stream, around a bend, down a six-foot embankment, then stopped. Ahead, Canzonari lay flat on a rock to drink from the stream. Seeing Bolan, he rolled away, fired once and ran.

The Beretta spat out a 3-shot volley, and Bolan saw one bullet hit the hood's left arm.

Joey screamed. The sound faded as he vanished into a clump of maples.

Bolan jumped over a fallen log, and dropped to a crouch behind a young cedar. Joey was circling now. Bolan pursued the sounds, stopping every few feet to listen.

For ten minutes Bolan tracked his quarry deeper into the woods, finally spotting him briefly as he worked across a bald area of shale along a small ridge. Except to get over ravines and ridges, the young creep was doing as little climbing or descending as possible.

Twenty minutes later Bolan spotted him sitting against a fir. The guy was panting, near exhaustion. He sat with his handgun up, watching his backtrack.

Bolan worked around him, then aimed and fired the Beretta at the guy's weapon hand. The slug slammed into the slide just over Joey's trigger finger, ripping the .32 from his hand.

He roared in pain, then jumped up and stumbled

toward the downed weapon, looking for his attacker. He tripped and almost fell. He did not recover the small gun in the leaves and ferns. He bellowed in anger and plunged forward into brush and out of Bolan's sight.

Then he screamed.

The Executioner rushed over and looked. He saw only Oregon sky and a cliff. Twenty feet below, Joey had landed in soft dirt and brush. He staggered to his feet and ran into deep cover.

But he was making no attempt to hide his trail, which swung around and headed back toward the highway. Bolan figured that hadn't been planned. He realized that the younger Canzonari was injured and lost.

The terrain became a rocky and barren slope again, and Bolan saw signs of recent lightning fire. He was halfway across the slope when a rock rolled down ahead of him. Then came another and another.

Bolan looked upward and saw the flash of a shirt as more boulders crashed down the slope toward the Executioner, each dislodging others. Soon a minor rockslide was thundering toward Bolan.

There was no time to outrun it. Bolan darted behind the closest tree. It was barely two feet thick, but it prevented the heavy rocks from hitting him.

After the last rock rolled by in a cloud of dirt and pebbles, Bolan leaped forward and raced around the slope in time to see his target leave a cleared section and enter heavy timber again not far from the highway.

Bolan ran faster now, fired his .44 AutoMag twice just to let Joey know he was still around.

In the heavy timber, Bolan heard the sounds ahead. The sounds of exhaustion, gasping and coughing. He came around a bend in the trail. A few steps later, the Executioner stopped.

The chase was over.

Joey Canzonari lay on the ground, exhausted. He struggled to sit up when he saw Bolan before him. The mobster's face was bright pink from the exertion. Sweat dripped from his nose and chin. His hair was wet and plastered against his head.

"You going to blow me away?"

"Why not? Isn't that the way you made your bones?"

"I'm only a bookkeeper and a computer man."

"Yeah, one of the innocents. And your hobby is killing girls and importing submachine guns for fun and profit."

"Who the hell cares?"

"Right. You have bigger worries. Like trying to convince me that you did not help torture Charleen."

"I don't know what you're talking about."

Canzonari clutched his wounded right hand with his left, sliding both of them toward his ankle. Bolan seemed not to notice the movement.

"So what do we do now?" Joey glared at the Executioner.

Bolan lowered the 93-R. "Up to you. Do you want to go back and face smuggling charges on the guns?"

"Look, there's enough money for you to live like a prince for the rest of your life. Five million dollars!"

"You don't have that much, Joey."

"My father does. He can get it for you."

Suddenly Joey pulled a snub-nosed .38 from an ankle holster.

The weapon barely cleared leather when Bolan lifted the Beretta and fired at the Mafia gunman.

The round slammed through Joey Canzonari's right cheekbone and was deflected upward into his brain. He dropped the .38 and fell against the blood-splattered fir. A gray-brown pulpy mess spilled from his shattered head.

Bolan stared a moment, his finger still on the trigger. Then he walked away from the corpse and slowly slid the 93-R back in leather.

The Executioner deduced his bearings from the snow-capped side of Mount Hood and walked back toward the cars.

Fifteen minutes later he saw Joey's car. On the front seat was an attaché case filled with money, probably some kind of downpayment on the submachine guns. It would make a good deposit in The Executioner's war chest. He threw the case in the crew wagon he had driven out and started toward Portland.

He drove to the Portland International Airport and parked outside the chopper service.

"Coming up in the world," Scooter Roick commented, eyeing the Caddy.

"Belongs to a friend of mine."

The pilot chuckled.

"Hey, looks like your little boat ride turned out fine."

"Fair. You have any problems?"

"Not yet."

Bolan tossed him a stack of hundreds from the attaché case. "Here's a little bonus for you."

"Must be at least five thousand dollars here! Anytime you need a jockey, call me!"

Bolan waved, got in the rented Thunderbird he had parked there that morning and put the attaché case and his weapons on the seat beside him.

Heading downtown, the Executioner considered his enemy: the Mafia, an international organization of the lowest and most cold-bloodedly violent criminals in the world. Many lives before, he had vowed to wipe them out, or at least thin their ranks.

The Executioner knew that a well-placed bullet, indeed, a stray, could finish his own life anytime. He was flesh and blood, and one faltered step would spell the end.

But until then he would never waver in his mission, launched in anger as a vendetta to avenge his family. But Bolan had long ago understood that personal hatred had no place in his quest, and that his fight had become a commitment to duty and justice.

For Mack Bolan, other people's fear of death was a weapon in itself. Unleashed against the Mafia organization, the fear could tear it apart, create gaps large enough for The Executioner to move in and wipe out the Mob.

The warrior's conflict had taken him to many states of the Union, and also to diverse foreign shores. During the terrorist wars he had even struck at the heart of the hydra, Moscow.

Now here he was, in a place where the land was truly bigger than man; where the majestic beauty of the Northwest seemed to humble ordinary mortals.

Bolan's rental neared the hotel, and as he entered the ramp of the underground parking garage, the Executioner put his past behind him and thought no more about it.

The present required all of his attention.

For the sake of any future at all.

16

Bolan took the elevator to his room. He had no sooner kicked off his shoes when there was a knock on the door. Bolan snarced the 93-R and moved against the wall next to the door.

"Who is it?" he asked.

"Johnny."

Bolan relaxed a fraction, slipped the chain off the catch and turned the knob to let his brother in.

Johnny was waving a newspaper.

"Look at this, guy."

"Read it to me," Bolan said, relocking the door and unfastening his weapons gear. Then he moved to the bed.

"The FBI has discovered a big cache of smuggled guns, worth over three million dollars, in a shipment of industrial machinery at a Gresham farm equipment dealership," Johnny read. "The military-type automatic weapons, rockets and launchers have been turned over to the Forty-first Division of the Oregon National Guard, and the rest is being held by the FBI.

"Gresham police are unable to account for the small-scale war that took place in the farm-equipment firm warehouse where the guns were

found. By the time firemen and police reached the
scene the exchange was over. Automatic weapons
and hand grenades had been used, and police report
men killed and wounded.

"Survivors claimed that some of the munitions in
the shipment blew up. However, police pointed out
that most of the wounded were hit by bullets, not
shrapnel. A large number of shell casings were also
found in the warehouse, many of the 9mm parabel-
lum size, as well as .45 and .38 caliber."

Johnny read another story about a Japanese ship
captain reporting a hijack attempt on his ship when a
group of men overpowered the river pilot and board-
ed along with him at Astoria. The captain reported
he and his crew had killed or pushed overboard all
five invaders. Neither the police nor the captain
could explain the attack.

Johnny smiled grimly and turned to the Executioner.

Mack Bolan was fast asleep.

Johnny Bolan let the newspaper drop to the floor
as he studied his big brother. Sadness assailed him as
he reflected on the tribulations of this brave warrior.
The younger Bolan wondered what path Mack's life,
indeed, the lives of the entire Bolan clan, would have
taken had circumstances not been as they were.

17

Bolan awoke with a start, muttering April Rose's name. He took in his surroundings, then looked at his watch.

"Damn," he said, strapping on his weapons. He had unfinished business in Portland.

Downstairs in the rented Thunderbird he checked over his equipment. A plan for dealing with Gino Canzonari, the Portland Godfather, had been forming in his mind.

He drove to a convenient phone booth and called Canzonari's private line, an unlisted number that changed every thirty days. The Godfather himself answered.

"Joey, is that you?" the father asked, obviously worried.

"No, this isn't Joey, but I know where he is. Interested, Canzonari?"

Bolan held the phone away from his ear when a roaring scream blasted through the receiver.

"Bolan, you bastard! Where is my son?"

"How much is he worth to you?"

"Half a million! I'll get you half a million in cash, no traces."

"Joey offered me one million."

"Okay, okay. That's the most I can get on short notice."

"Deal. In an attaché case. Come alone. Anyone with you or following you, and Joey is turkey meat."

"Yes, yes. Don't get excited. This is just a business deal. Money for the boy."

"My terms. Go to Killingsworth and Thirty-third. Be there at exactly 2:00 P.M. From there you'll get new instructions."

"Whaddya mean, 'new instructions'? Joey better be with you."

"He won't be. I've got to make sure nobody is following you and you don't have the place staked out. Take it or leave it."

"I'll be there. I'll drive myself. Satisfied?"

"At two." Bolan hung up.

THE EXECUTIONER RECOGNIZED THE MAN walking along the sidewalk from pictures he had seen. He was about five-five and 250 pounds, and carried an attaché case.

Gino Canzonari was doing as he was told.

Bolan moved his car slowly behind the Mafia chieftain. He could spot no suspicious cars trailing the Don. He might have kept his word—doubtful, but possible.

The Executioner pulled half a car-length ahead of the man and motioned him to get in. The Beretta was trained on the Mob chieftain all the way.

"Canzonari, take off your suit coat," Bolan commanded.

Canzonari hesitated, then stripped it off.

"Now take off your shirt." As soon as the mobster opened it, Bolan saw the wires and the small radio transmitter. He jerked the apparatus off Canzonari, threw it out the window and hit the gas.

Bolan noticed the unmarked police car behind him, and another on Killingsworth. He flattened the Thunderbird's gas pedal and the big car surged on. He slid through a stoplight, wound north to Lombard and Union and was soon on the 99 freeway heading across the Columbia into Washington State, toward Seattle. His gun was trained on Canzonari all the time.

He exited on the Washington side, powered around two interchanges and finally parked below an overpass.

Canzonari scowled. "Cops made me wear the wire. They heard about you and about Joey missing. They made me do it!"

"Sure they did." Bolan frisked him quickly, found a .38 in an ankle holster and threw it out the window. "They made you wear that, too? Where are the rest of your boys? How many cars did you have following us?"

"Two, but you lost them."

"You bring the money?"

Canzonari pointed to the attaché case.

"Good. Now you can tell me what happened to Charlotte Albers."

"Who?"

"Charlotte Albers and her twin sister, Charleen Granger. Two pretty black girls about twenty-five."

"Granger...yes, the black girl. I hear she died up in the park."

"Your men killed her, Canzonari, and used her for
bait to get me. But they missed. I don't miss."

Bolan edged out from under the concrete overpass
and turned south back toward Oregon. He drove
with the flow of traffic—heavier now, nearing rush
hour—figuring the cops would not be watching close
enough.

Eventually he turned off, heading along the
Columbia River on the Oregon side. At Troutdale he
turned south until he picked up U.S. 26, which
became the Mount Hood Loop highway route.

"Where the hell we going?" Canzonari asked.

"I thought you wanted to see Joey."

"You got him stashed up here?"

"Right."

They drove in silence until they passed Brightwood. At the spot where he had run Joey's car off
the road, Bolan pulled to the shoulder.

"Out. We're taking a walk." Bolan locked the
Thunderbird, moved Canzonari across the road, and
they plunged into the timber.

"What the hell?"

Ten minutes later Bolan motioned Canzonari
around a pair of tall fir trees and pointed.

Joey lay where Bolan had left him. Canzonari ran
forward. He dropped to his knees and grabbed his
son's body, rocking back and forth. Then he jumped
up and charged Bolan. The Executioner sidestepped
him, tripped him and pushed the fat hoodlum to the
ground.

"You bastard! You promised me my son back!"

"I said I'd bring you to him and I did. Just think

of Joey as payment for Charleen Granger. You killed her, and now your son is dead.''

Canzonari rushed at him again. Bolan slammed the Beretta across the mobster's head, smashing him to the ground.

''There's still payment due from you for Charlotte Albers, Canzonari. We'll think of some way to even the scales. Now pick up your son and carry him back to the road.''

Dusk had settled as Canzonari stumbled to the edge of the highway with the dead weight. He collapsed there. A car rolled by, and Bolan ducked out of sight.

Canzonari got to his knees and stared at his dead son.

Then he turned, producing a blade, and lunged at the Executioner's throat. Bolan drew Big Thunder and pulled the trigger.

The boom of the .44 AutoMag shattered the silence of the forest. The heavy lead slug caught Canzonari squarely in the heart with such force that the man's torso exploded. The smoking remains fell to the ground beside the dead youth.

Bolan held the big gun steady, then slowly lowered and holstered it. Canzonari's demise had not been planned, but the Executioner was not sorry about this unexpected turn. Someone would find them come daylight.

Bolan crouched as a car passed, then ran across the dark highway to the Thunderbird and drove back to Sandy Boulevard. He could not find an open car-rental agency so he continued to one on the outskirts of Portland, left the car and took his suitcase of weapons and the attaché case of money. The Portland police would not be able to trace the Thunderbird back to him.

He changed taxis three times, then walked two blocks with the suitcase to the hotel.

When the Executioner stepped into the hotel lobby, Johnny jumped from a chair and took the suitcase and attaché case without a word. Nor did the two speak in the crowded elevator.

As they walked down the hall toward their room, Bolan told his younger brother, "We're finished here. Time to move on."

18

But it was not that easy. Bolan felt burdened by his war, pulled down by the gravity of his fearful commitment. The Executioner's mood was turning dark, and so it was that he began to think of Johnny in the renewed light of protectiveness.

Johnny had said he wanted to show Bolan the updated plans for his strongbase down in Del Mar. Bolan decided to go along with the kid.

He'd drive down from Los Angeles in the coming days and take time out to check into this strengthened strongbase with him. Then maybe he could talk to the kid. Dammit, he *would* talk to the kid.

And, dammit, Johnny was no kid, as was evidenced every time the young man clenched his jaw when he saw street signs in Portland that read "Sandy." This was a battle-hardened young adult.

Much as Bolan tried to prevent it, after a couple of days his heavy mood finally got to Johnny. The two Bolans were driving down Route 5, Johnny at the wheel, cruising through San Clemente and south past the Marine Corps base at Camp Pendleton on their left, the midday sun burning above the rental car, their elbows stuck out of open windows. It was hot, the breeze dry and bitter with fumes, but both men preferred it to the air-conditioning.

"What's up with you, Mack? You haven't said a word since L.A." Johnny looked over at his brother.

Bolan grunted.

Johnny persisted. "Want a cigarette? I know you're out because I saw you smoke your last one."

"You don't smoke."

"But I carry a couple of packs in my bags," Johnny said, "for just such occasions as this."

"I don't want your cigarettes." Bolan looked out of the passenger window, through the blustery air of sun-smitten dust and exhaust particles, and what he saw was far, far away.

"I don't understand you," Johnny said. "You just ripped open and rubbed out the entire underbelly of Portland, Oregon, and now you're down in the dumps."

"I did what?"

"Sorry to get poetic," Johnny said. "Let me put it another way. You trashed the loan files of finance companies, you scoured the streets of the east side of Portland, you busted a family-owned gun store under the Ross Island bridge approach, then hit the fancy Washington Heights district—"

"I know," Bolan muttered. "I was there too."

"—And you crushed an old man's bad bones into. . .into the dust and disgrace of his own son!"

"Now you *are* getting poetic," The Executioner said. "I'll lighten up if you will."

"It's a deal. But I just don't see how you can feel

blue after successfully hijacking an already hijacked ship."

"I guess you could say we did just that."

"Sure we did. Not only that, you also busted up an arms shipment landing that would've made the Mafia the biggest goddamn gun dealer in the nation."

Bolan raised his left hand gently for some quiet.

Johnny could see that his brother was still troubled. The young man decided not to push it.

They turned off the main highway before they reached the little coastal community of Del Mar and wound down the street next to the water, then doubled back around a canyon that sliced through to the sea. Near the top of the double-back, a lane led off the street. It had been blacktopped recently and blocking the way was an electrically operated lift gate.

Johnny put a card in a slot in the metal box. The gate arm swung up.

He drove down the hundred-foot-long lane, crowded on both sides by eucalyptus trees. There were no other houses on the lane.

From the outside the strongbase looked like any other beach home, slightly smaller than a real weekender, but as big as a cottage could be on the restricted site. The ravine dropped off sharply beside the roadway and on the other side of the house a forty-foot cliff went straight down to the breakers. There was no garage, but a carport had been built over the blacktop against the lane side of the house.

Bolan looked around. From the driveway and the cottage, not another house was visible. Now and then someone might brave the rubble to walk past the rock falls on the tiny beach, but not often.

"I like it here," Bolan said. "Show me the inside."

The door had two locks, two dead bolts with inchlong prongs set into case hardened steel boxes, strapped into the special four-by-four that was built into the doorjamb.

Inside, the younger Bolan gave his famous brother a tour of Strongbase One.

Johnny was proud of what he had done to the place. Two walls upstairs had been torn out and the area turned into storage space. The ground level housed utilities and kitchen, and in the basement was the communications room.

"Everything you see is standardized Radio Shack," Johnny announced, showing off the basement's disorderly array of computer hardware. "These four modems, working on a one-always-on basis, are linked to the electronic bulletin board on the end wall. That board is programmed to display and interact with several key alert situations. I've got about twelve such alerts listed already." As he spoke Johnny touched a switch and twelve horizontal slots on the board lit up with rapidly changing code numbers; two screens flickered to life below the board. "And the computers can parallel and anticipate real-life situations. Something like having a second nervous system."

"What sort of linkup?" Bolan asked.

"We're hooked up with one of the satellites that Kurtzman's being using," Johnny replied. "A relatively low power transmission gives me two-way voice radio with you anywhere in the U.S. For incoming telephone calls, we have a triple dead drop that goes from East to West Coast, back to East and then back here again. That way the calls cannot be traced—by the phone company or by anybody else. We have dual recorders on voice actuation, so you can talk for up to sixty minutes without a break if you want to send recorded transmissions."

"I've got to talk to you about this, Johnny."

Ignoring Bolan, Johnny ran upstairs to fetch two attaché cases he had brought inside from the car. As he returned with them he said, "There's a million and a half in greenbacks in these two cases, Mack. That's just from the Canzonari operation. I've collected six other cases like these from your other recent hits. The contents have been stashed in four separate banks and invested in money market funds. So there's no shortage of cash."

"That's not my concern," Bolan said. "You've done a magnificent job here, Johnny. I'll be happy to fund whatever—"

"I knew you'd come around," Johnny interrupted eagerly. "This place can be a link with Stony Man back East, Mack. Don't you see? This is a vital point in one huge triangle—Phoenix Force and Able Team at Stony Man Farm in Virginia, me at Strongbase One in Del Mar and you, Mack, out there—"

"Wait a minute, Johnny-O, we really do have to talk." With that, Bolan put a strong arm around Johnny's shoulder and led him up the stairs.

In the kitchen, without saying a word, he sat his

brother down on a chair at a table by the big window. The sunlight streaming outside illuminated the peaceful beauty that surrounded them, but the kitchen was cool and in shade.

Bolan went to the refrigerator and fished out two beers. The place was well stocked for the kind of afternoon Bolan had in mind.

"I'm going to tell you a story," he began, sitting across from his brother and opening his beer. "I've been feeling bad, Johnny. I'm not good with words, but I'm going to tell you something. I'm going to sketch out something that happened to me. You'll have to fill in some of the spaces yourself. You'll have to flesh it out because I don't have the words. But it's something that happened to me before mom and pop and Cindy were killed. Back in Nam. The story has a moral, I guess you could call it, and that's why I'm telling it to you now."

Johnny Bolan pushed away his beer and looked at Mack. The Executioner's presence filled the room.

"Whatever it was I accomplished in Portland," Bolan said, "I accomplished it far, far too late. To you, we were in Portland to hit the Mafia and the terrorists, to avenge Sandy Darlow and April Rose. But I was there for something else."

"What?"

Bolan's voice grew calmer, deeper. "I was there to take my revenge on all the councils of kings. To shove it down their throats one last time. When I think of my buddy...when I see a picture of him in my mind, of my buddy back in Nam, I think of you, Johnny."

As the afternoon drew on, Johnny Bolan heard what it was that Mack Bolan had learned in Vietnam and what it was that made him fight for friendship to such an extent that now he could not bear to expose his younger brother to any of the dangers of the Executioner's world.

To Johnny it was an accounting for events that reached their true conclusion only days ago in Portland. Bolan told the tale in brief, urgent, first-person snatches of image and commentary. But the effect on Johnny's imagination was complete and everlasting.

This is the story Mack Bolan told his brother.

19

Dusk turned the jungle to an eerie, formless gray. A breeze whispered through the treetops. He had come to know the jungle as a living thing, a breathing thing that gave up no dead.

Bolan let his thoughts slip away, and listened below the faint rustling of leaves.

He stopped beside a thicket. A scraping sound slipped through the leaves around him. He eased the AR to full auto and searched for movement. The jungle surrounded him, held him, breaking his vision with a confusion of vegetation that sighed almost imperceptibly in the pale darkness. Where the hell was Buddy?

Bolan eased himself back a step. The scraping sound came from behind. Bolan turned in painfully slow motion, the AR's snout moving with him. The jungle was still.

It was Buddy. He was squatting beside a pool of black water that reflected the deepening, broken sky. Connecticut was gone from Buddy. Mack Bolan looked back a million years at the small man squatting in the swamp, shaving his head with a knife.

"Don't do it, Buddy."

"I'm done for, Mack."

"No, you're not." Bolan was crouched beside him. They talked four inches apart. Buddy scraped his head with his killing knife, shaving the hairs from the scalp, but leaving a full swath from brow to nape. The Mohawk. Bolan wanted to stay his hand, stop the shaving, as if that would alter Buddy's fate—but Bolan did not want his throat slit.

Buddy shaved and talked in a shaky voice. An orange spider emerged from behind his ear and crawled carefully down his neck.

"I smelled Leslie today. No, really. All of a sudden it just hit me. It was like she was beside me. Can you believe I gave her up to do a second tour? Man, I smelled her hair, her skin." Buddy was lost in himself, talking unevenly as he shaved. "You want to hear something even crazier? I had this memory, finally, of my mother, like I've never been able to remember her. She died when I was three. But today I remembered her giving me a bath."

"Buddy? What was in the letter you got this morning?" asked Bolan, though he already knew.

Buddy swallowed but continued shaving, as if by rote. The spider, which had crawled so carefully down his neck, rode Buddy's Adam's apple as he swallowed, but then danced in alarm as the water came trickling down from Buddy's head.

"Oh, you know. Leslie, ah—" he swallowed again "—Leslie got herself a Jody. I knew it would happen."

"Buddy, you've got to remember—"

"Only regret I have is that I won't be coming back to cut his frigging balls off," Buddy said to no one as he rinsed the short hairs from his blade. It was Buddy's trademark—the knife that was supersharp but dark. It reflected no light. Bolan could hardly see Buddy now. Their whispers hissed in the half light.

"You're doing the Mohawk because of Jody? That's not like you."

"It's not Jody, man. It's this fucking mission. I got this feeling. First we go to penetrate the village that Intelligence says is a VC camp, and it ain't. Just a bunch of goddamn villagers. Did you see those little kids with the water buffalo? If you hadn't called off the air strike they'd be dead meat. And then we hump it to the next village and there's no VC there, either. Then I got that smell and my mother, and I see myself in the water, and I get hit with this feeling— Buddy, you're a dead man. Time for the Mohawk. Buddy's going to die in the Mekong."

Bolan watched as Buddy rose on his haunches. He was sweating like a pig, staring at the jungle. Beads of sweat on his forehead and brow reflected the last touches of light. His left hand hung down to the muck, clutching the blade. Bolan saw Buddy's nostrils quivering. A Mohawk meant you weren't coming back. He wanted Buddy before he slipped away any farther.

"That's a beautiful Mohawk, Buddy."

"You think so?"

"Can I make a suggestion?"

"Sure."

"Spread some mud on your scalp. It's shining white."

Buddy reached into the muck and looked at it as

though reading the entrails of his own corpse. Slowly he raised his hands to his scalp and worked the swamp muck on either side of the stripe of chestnut hair.

When finished he looked up at Mack Bolan as if his mind were made up all the more. Keeping his hollow eyes fixed on Bolan, he lifted the cord that hung around his neck and gathered it in his hand.

"Here. I want you to have this."

He reached over and put the tangle in Bolan's palm. A human ear hung from the cord, limp and leathery.

"My first kill. It's yours."

"I don't want this," said Bolan. "Never have."

"Take it."

"No."

Bolan saw the look on Buddy's face and put the ear in his pocket. They moved off, with Buddy walking point.

The darkness grew wet with rain.

They crawled into position just as the moon was sinking behind the scrub. Before them lay the enemy camp, a hillock among the mangroves that was honeycombed with tunnels and caves. It looked to be a full fifty yards across the top.

This jungle would hide an army forever. The delta was fingered with ridges that rose from the primeval swamp, covered in scrub oak and nettles in an endless, unbroken cover of vegetation. The VC gathered and struck their targets when and where they chose, always melting away into the delta. There was no way of destroying them without destroying the delta itself.

The young Sergeant Bolan had picked up a Washington newspaper with the Pentagon's account of areas controlled by American and RV forces. He found it a cruel joke. The allies never held any position more than temporarily, and then only as long as their firepower blasted anything that moved. The VC owned the night, anywhere and anytime they wanted to collect.

Buddy and Bolan watched the occasional movements of VC in the camp, trying to make out where the tunnels began and ended. There were too many entrances to count.

"I think we hit the jackpot," Buddy said.

"I stopped counting at ten."

"This is a hard-core regiment. These guys aren't farming by day."

"Probably sitting on enough ammo and supplies for the whole quadrant," muttered Bolan. "We can't do this alone. We'll do a sapper job on the place, then call in the choppers once the action starts."

"You do the perimeter, Mack. I'm going in to see if I can blow the ammo. Meet by that trail in an hour and a half."

Bolan was about to say, "no, I'll go in," but Buddy had already slipped into the swamp that lay at the foot of the ridge.

Bolan gave him five minutes and then snaked in himself. He felt the cool touch of the water as it slipped through his fatigues and surrounded his body. With only his eyes above the waterline, Bolan crawled toward the camp. The moon had set.

Bolan eased every thought from his mind. He was

empty. He let everything of himself slip away. He reduced himself to a presence. The water passed through him. He became pure killer.

Where the ridge rose from the swamp, Bolan slowed to almost imperceptible movement. In his mind he was Buddy's blade—a death that reflected no light. He rose from the water so slowly he could feel the evaporation from his neck. Every nerve was vacant yet highly aware. Ten feet away two guards sat in a shallow hole, looking at him.

Bolan's crawl toward them was agonizingly slow. They looked directly at him but could not see his form in the dark swamp. Bolan saw the outline of rifles in their laps.

Bolan lowered each hand carefully as he crawled, testing the surface before he let his weight press on it. He covered four feet in ten minutes.

An eternity passed. One of the guards moved his head, sending an alarm along the swamp crawler's spine. Bolan's hand came down slowly on something plastic. A claymore.

Bolan could smell the guards. He was five feet from their hole. He began to turn the claymore around, five degrees at a time, so that it faced the guards.

One guard turned to the other and spoke in a whisper. The second guard sat up listening, the claymore wires in his hands.

Bolan stopped breathing when he saw the wires. His lungs began to burn. His heart pounded audibly in his ears. Three feet away the guard's knees shifted in the blackness.

Nothing more was said. The two guards listened intently.

Bolan finished rotating the claymore and moved off into the blackness. Then he turned two more.

Time was running out. Bolan finished the perimeter after an agonizing hour and then crawled into the camp to meet Buddy.

Bolan felt Buddy's breath before he heard him. The voice came in his ear, barely perceptible.

"I found the commander. He's copying something down on his map as the radioman gets it. They're giving out the locations of the VC regiments."

"Did you hear any of it?"

"Hear it? I'm going for the map, Mack."

"You've got a pair of brass balls, my friend."

"I always knew I'd die in this shit hole."

Buddy slid off before Bolan could say anything more. Bolan's guts went cold.

Bolan crouched by the trail, knife in hand. He felt a centipede scamper up his leg, but remained motionless. It was not worth risking exposure to kill it. He could feel it work its way into his crotch.

A cry went up within the tunnels the instant that Buddy returned silently to Bolan's position. Someone had found the dead commander and radioman.

Adrenaline coursed through the two Americans as they ran away from the trail, into the brush. A claymore blew, sending a flash and a bizarre shadow through the foliage. Then another, and a scream, and then the ARs opened up. The VC were shooting at one another and the Americans were escaping through the perimeter. The firefight reared its head around them, cutting the jungle to tatters. Bolan jumped, doubled over, across a thicket, then heard Buddy grunt. He turned back, saw something that looked like Buddy on the ground, and then the VC rained heavy machine-gun fire across the distance that separated them.

Bolan crawled under the fire and grabbed Buddy's elbow, dragging him through a pool of viscous muck, part of which was Buddy's own vomit. The enemy were firing from two directions now; a crisscross of angry slugs whined hotly past in bright flashes.

Bolan picked up Buddy and ran as fast as his legs could pump. There was too much confusion to hear anything. He crashed through the brush with Buddy's guts leaking down his back.

"The dirty bastards," Buddy was chanting. "This dirty fucking war!" Finally he sank to his knees by the radio.

Bolan had circled to find the radio, and was breathless. He keyed the set quickly. He could hear the VC following the trail of Buddy's blood. They would be on top of him soon. With one hand over Buddy's mouth, Bolan gave the coordinates for an artillery hit, followed by another set for the Medevac. Then he lifted the radio and Buddy and staggered away.

On the next ridge Bolan sat with the radio calling the coordinates again. From far off he heard the booming of the big guns, then the blasts that shook his stomach as the big shells staggered up the ridge.

"East fifty...north thirty..." Bolan was waiting for the big one. The shell that would blow that

ammo. "North another thirty," he said, and then it
went. The sky cracked open. Bolan and Buddy lay
side by side as the ground bucked beneath the roiling
fireball. In the reflection of Buddy's glazed eyes
Bolan saw the flames blossom.

"BUDDY DIDN'T MAKE IT, Mack," said Crawford.
The lieutenant colonel was Bolan's commanding
officer, but every man in Penetration Team Able was
the CO's equal as far as Crawford was concerned.
"He caught too many slugs. Too damn many."
    The sun had risen, turning the shack into a steam
bath. A portable fan blew fetid air at them. Bolan's
eyes burned like coals.
    "Where is he?"
    "They shipped him out. He's going back to the
States in a bag. Still has a father alive, I think."
    Bolan said nothing. Crawford offered him a ciga-
rette and then lit it for him.
    "I'm not going on the next mission."
    "Mack, we've all lost friends."
    "I don't mean that. Buddy went in after a map he
saw the commander drawing on. I bet he's still got
it."
    "No way. I emptied his pockets myself. Nothing.
Except the letter from home."
    "Then he swallowed it."
    "Mack, come on now—"
    "No way. Buddy knew he was going home in a
bag.... A field map is made of canvas and paper.
The part of it that Buddy swallowed could still be un-
dissolved in his stomach right now."

Crawford was about to reply, but said nothing. It was true about Buddy knowing he was going to die, of course. Everyone had seen the Mohawk. He tapped a pencil nervously on the desk.

"Let me call down to Saigon. I have a friend who works—"

Bolan cut him off. "I'm doing this personally. No more depending on someone else who doesn't care."

Crawford sighed wearily. "All right. This is going to take a lot of Vaseline. A lot." Crawford picked up the telephone and said to Mack, "Get a fresh uniform." Then, "Get me Colonel Winters."

THE CHOPPER LANDED with a lurch. That was what Nam felt like to Bolan, just as the lurch of a pickup was what New England felt like. He stepped out and looked across the tarmac at the depot, an immense corrugated metal structure shining in the bright sun like an airplane hangar. Beyond it a transport lifted off, the heat of its exhaust turning the surrounding jungle into a shimmering blob of green. The depot was temporary; the jungle would win it back. Bolan never looked at the jungle without thinking about its inevitable victory.

The office jutted out from the side of the depot like an unwanted appendage. Everyone wore clean crisp uniforms. The place was calm, but eerie in its calmness; Bolan wanted out, though he did not give himself that choice.

He walked in and explained his visit to a fresh-looking kid from Alabama. Then he waited for someone with authority. On the radio an English voice was singing about sympathy and the Devil. Bolan resisted the urge to crush the radio under his boot. This was the rear. This was how it was back here. He wanted out more than ever.

Ten minutes later a man came to the office in a white coat. He looked like a New York cabdriver, but spoke in educated tones.

"Dr. Morgan," he said, reaching out a hand. "What's the problem?"

Bolan explained. He needed to locate a corpse. There might be some vital intel within the body itself. As he talked they entered the depot. Bolan was hit by the coldness of the air. Then he understood—air-conditioning. He hadn't felt it in . . . how long? A past life.

"What's the name and serial number?"

Bolan withdrew the slip of paper from his pocket and read the serial number. They were standing in a giant warehouse divided by rack upon rack of dead GIs in plastic bags. The racks went down the length of the room, parallel, chilling. A thousand dead eyes staring through milky plastic at the ceiling. The predominant smell was of disinfectant.

"You see, a piece of canvas and paper like that would ninety-nine times in a hundred be lost. We have to remove the viscera from the body and then stuff the cavity with cotton soaked in formaldehyde. There's no way we could ship them otherwise. And all that junk goes down into the bins for disposal."

Morgan called to another whitecoat talking to a private in uniform. They came over and the grunt was sent to locate Buddy. The other doctor doubted they would have seen such a piece of paper. They told

Bolan about their careers as coroners back home. Bolan did not respond.

The grunt called them over and stood waiting with cap in hand, pointing to a long bag on a wheeled stretcher. Morgan unzipped the top of the bag. Bolan looked down at Buddy's face.

"This one's done. You do this one, Mike?"

"I can't remember. Sergeant, this one's already done. I guess you're a little late."

Bolan looked down at the bag. Buddy's Mohawk was sticking up beyond the folds of the plastic.

"Cut him open again. I have to be sure."

"Are you crazy? We already took his guts out."

"Cut him open again."

"Sergeant, you don't seem to understand—"

"It's you who doesn't understand, doctor. Get your goddamn knife out, or I'll do it myself."

Morgan turned to the grunt. "Get the guards. This crazy asshole needs cooling off."

The grunt keyed the walkie-talkie and called for guards. Bolan fumed. "Morgan, your ass is on the line for this."

A door flew open at the far end of the room. Two MPs trotted in, bats at the ready.

"Sergeant," the doctor said to Bolan, "you'd better watch what you say, or you'll go home in a plastic uniform, too."

BOLAN WAITED for the transport to lift off into the night. Then he vaulted the fence. The depot was not exactly a high security area. He crossed the tarmac without seeing anyone.

The doors at the loading bay were still open. Bolan walked in as if he belonged there. He saw only grunts. This was probably a new shift.

Inside the storage area he felt again the coolness. The song about the Devil would not leave his head. Without hesitation, Bolan climbed into a forklift and motored down the aisles to the spot where Buddy lay. He checked the serial number of the bag's ID tag and lifted the body onto the pallet of the forklift. Then he motored to the side of the room.

Bolan worked hidden by the forklift. He unzipped the bag, bracing himself against the stench of putre-faction. Buddy stared up at him from a drained face. His skin was a dull grayish green, cold and sagging. Dried mud clung to his scalp. Bolan wondered about the person welcoming Buddy home. They would never understand what was about to happen.

Bolan forced open the jaws and looked inside. It was an ugly purple-black hole that stank. Nothing.

He took the knife from his pocket and held it to Buddy's neck where the crude stitches began. Buddy's sightless eyes stared at him, his Mohawk stark on his scalp. Bolan closed Buddy's eyes.

He sank the knife into the dead throat and pulled. Buddy's eyes popped open.

Quickly Bolan drew the knife downward to the belly and watched the flesh part along the broken stitches. He separated the flesh and stared in shock.

Bags of white powder sat gleaming among the gray-pink cavity of Buddy's corpse.

Bolan broke one open and tasted it. Heroin.

The vulgarity of it made Bolan sick. In a daze he closed the bag, put it back on the shelf and left.

For once in his life Bolan was too sickened to think.

BOLAN SAT in a Saigon bar, trying to get Buddy's face to go away, but wherever he looked he saw it. The bar radio called mockingly from home. The songs would never sound the same for him. He hated them, now and forever. Rage was twisting his guts into a knot.

Three GIs sat on beat-up chairs at a table, crushing beer cans. The ceiling fan crisscrossed them with shadows as they talked at one another of their sexual exploits.

Bolan drowned out their boasting. He had to consider his options: the local police, who were in the pay of the VC or the smugglers or both; the American Military Police, who could just about tie their shoes and swing a bat and not much else; the Division command; or the CIA. Bolan chose the most powerful people in the country: the CIA.

He went to the telephone just as two Vietnamese girls entered the room. Bolan paused momentarily. They were identical twins, both petite and slender and lovely. He heard a whistle from the GIs and watched the girls ignore the whistle. Bolan telephoned.

He waited through the clicks and buzzes, and eventually got through to someone named Barker, who proceeded to question Bolan in a bored but probing way. Bolan was vague; Barker was feeling him out to see if he was a crazy.

Bolan went as far as he would go, then demanded an interview. Barker took down the location and said he would send someone over.

Bolan hung up and turned around. The GIs stood over the girls who stood mutely at the bar. The girls wanted to leave. The tallest of the GIs leaned down and beerily centered his red-rimmed eyes on one of the twins.

"You no-a like me, baby-san? You understand I want a little tail tonight?"

The GI drained his beer and said to the other, "I think I'm seein' double, Frank. Two fuckin' identical pieces of A-1 tail. Man oh man."

"Never liked slant-eyed pussy myself," said Frank, burping.

"Got no complaints about it myself," said the tall one. "So long as I'm sure it ain't dead." The girls tried to leave, but he grabbed them by their wrists. "Oh, hey, the party's just starting."

Bolan felt his hands twitch. He'd seen enough. "Let them go," he said, wearily.

The GIs turned to stare at the big bastard in the sergeant's uniform. Did he want these two women for himself? Conversation stopped; only the radio continued its mocking, something about someone was going to the chapel. . . .

"Come on, Sarge," said one of the GIs, pulling out cash from his pocket. "They're only slopes."

Rage ran through Bolan like electricity. His hands snaked apart, one clutching the GI's uniform at the neck, the other drawing back and then lashing him cruelly in the face. The GI dropped his money, his face running with blood, and sank to his knees.

His friend held him, tottering and bleeding, and looked up hotly at the big bastard standing over them. "What are you, a Commie or something?"

The bartender had called the MPs. Now he stood wiping nervously at the bar, half watching. The two GIs were busy trying to lift their friend from the dirty floor before the arrival of the pricks with the hats and bats.

A Jeep lurched to a stop outside the bar. Bolan turned; not the MPs, but a man in sunglasses with a whore. This would be the CIA contact, he guessed. They were the only people around here who wore sunglasses at night.

"You Bolan?" the man called out as he sat lazily in the Jeep. Neon flashed on him in red and blue. "I'm Naiman."

"Who the hell is she?" asked Bolan, climbing into the back of the Jeep.

"Don't worry, I'm just dropping her off."

Bolan looked at Naiman's whore. False eyelashes sat incongruously on her eyelids. She sucked a long cigarette. She probably spoke French. Yeah, she'd lain under a regiment of sweating officers and bureaucrats, first from France, then from America.

The whore ran her fingers down Naiman's neck as he drove through the streets. He shrugged to shake her off. She was whispering to him, increasing the force of her nails, digging them into his flesh. She wanted him to pick her up the next night. Naiman shook his head, motioning with his eyes to indicate the passenger in the back seat. She left off, insulted, and then said, "You not really a strong man like I said, Jim. You a mama's boy."

"Sure, sure," said Naiman, pulling the Jeep to a stop in front of a hovel. She got out, holding her snakeskin purse. Bolan could see through the fabric of her shirt that she wore a snakeskin bra to match. "Talk to you soon, Barbra-Ann."

Bolan climbed into the front seat. "Drive," he said.

They wheeled through the cool darkness. The time before dawn was the only time offering respite from the dreadful heat and humidity. In the stillness drifted the booming of far-off artillery. Saigon slipped past them, a dirty, hunched, downtrodden city. Gradually the density of dwellings thinned, and Bolan smelled the dew and the river.

Naiman pulled the Jeep into a gravel field between the railroad tracks and the river.

"Who was the guy I spoke to first?" asked Mack.

"I don't know. I got a call from the secretary. Why?"

"I don't like it. The fewer people who know about this thing the better."

"This thing being...?"

Bolan told him about the trouble with the coroner, Morgan, and then of cutting open Buddy and finding the bags of raw heroin. A transport plane roared overhead as they talked, wing lights streaking in the darkness. Another load of dead would be vibrating in its belly.

Naiman sighed, considering. He saw ramifications.

"You're right, Sergeant," he said, turning to look at Bolan. "The CIA has a duty to stop this. I don't know if I, personally, will handle the case—"

A crack split the air. Naiman's head blew apart, his forehead exploding in a wet spray that lashed Bolan's face.

Bolan rolled to the ground, gripping his Colt M16A1.

20

Slugs ripped into the Jeep with a scream of metal. Under the Jeep, Bolan watched the tires of the cars as they swung across the gravel toward him, spraying dirt and stones. Someone in the car was raking the Jeep with slugs, but the car's headlights were still not turned on.

Bolan rolled to the right, coming up with his submachine gun pointing to the car. From his right flank Bolan saw another car, and then they both jerked on their lights.

Bolan was caught like an animal in the blinding glare. He rolled again, dodging the killer slugs, and then with a steady stance blew the lights from the car ahead.

Slugs from the second car chewed the dirt, zipping up toward him. He aimed and took out the driver of the second car. The lights went crazy as the driver jerked the pedal to the floor and smashed into a post. Engines roared like hellions in the lonely yard. The first car was dark but still spitting slugs.

Bolan was in darkness now. He ran at the second car, its engine screaming futilely. Bolan veered when the door opened, and a gunman climbed out.

In the darkness Bolan just made out the chain-link

fence before he hit it. He vaulted in time, grunting, clawing for the top. Halfway over, fingers clawing through the wires, Bolan felt the fence shaking under the impact of the slugs. The vibrations stung his hands as the gunmen pasted the fence with fire.

Bolan dropped over and fell behind a stack of steel drums. Slugs cut through the metal.

Bolan waited for his pursuers to get closer.

With deep slow breaths he cut the pounding of his blood to a roar, and took aim. He saw that the gunmen wore suits. He selected a face and blew it apart. The second gunman dropped to the ground, bringing up an AR.

But Bolan had gone.

Splashes in the river were all that could be heard. The sounds retreated downriver.

BOLAN HEARD VOICES in the brightness. He woke and jumped up simultaneously, grabbing for his gun even before he knew where he was. The Colt was in his grasp as he blinked, trying to see who to kill. It was only children playing on the riverbank. God, one day a Nam vet was going to jump out of his sleep and kill his own kid before he realized he was no longer in Nam.

The sun was well above the horizon, the day already hot and oppressive. Bolan was coated in sweat as he crouched under a railway bridge. Twenty yards down the riverbank, a cluster of Vietnamese children were throwing rocks into the river. Bolan wiped sweat from his face and thought of the countless stones he had skipped into rivers as a child. Some things were universal for children, even in war. Pleasure came unexpectedly in this place.

The children were excitedly picking up stones from the bank, competing for some target that floated just at the surface of the water. Bolan watched as it drifted closer. The stones splashed into the water around it. The children were following it down with the current toward Bolan.

When it was fifteen yards away, Bolan saw what it was. The corpse floated feet first, puffy and discolored, stripped naked. The face was gone, blown away by a slug, but Bolan could tell the body was a Westerner's and not a Vietnamese's. A rock from one of the kids hit the chest with a hollow thump and bounced into the water. The child laughed; another threw up his arms in triumph. The rest went back upriver, throwing at a second body.

Bolan grabbed the kid by the arm. The kid practically jumped from his skin at the big guy's touch. He looked up in fear. Bolan addressed him in Vietnamese, asked him if he wanted to make some money for his family. The kid agreed cautiously. Bolan wrote out a Vietnamese name and an address in Saigon and handed the paper to him, along with some money. The young boy handed back the paper. He was illiterate. Bolan told him the name and address and had him repeat it to him. If he brought the man back with him there would be more money, but he must hurry and he must tell no one.

The child raced off. His friends were excited—more corpses were coming down. Bolan heard another thump.

The first corpse came closer to shore as it drifted under the bridge. Bolan waded in. The corpse passed from sunlight to shadow and its color emerged better: greenish-gray skin, purple on the underside where the blood had settled. Red hair—that would be important. Bolan pulled it into an eddy under the bridge. The face was unrecognizable.

The second corpse drifted headfirst. Bolan had to chase a buzzard off the face before it would give up its meal. Another head shot. Chestnut hair.

The third corpse was Vietnamese—shot in the chest, but the face had been hit and was swollen and distorted.

Naiman didn't come down the river. Bolan waited as the day grew hotter. The corpses swirled in the slow eddy, around and around like a kindergarten game. The sun was advancing across the eddy, and they would be well on their way to rotting in a few more hours. Bolan watched them go around and around, bobbing in the heat.

An hour later the boy returned with a Vietnamese man dressed in a white suit. Bolan gave the boy his money and sent him off.

"Vu Quoc Thanh. Thanks for coming."

"What do you want from me, Sergeant Bolan? I cannot help you in your position."

"What position is that?"

"You murdered Jim Naiman last night. They know you work for the VC. Every police force and intelligence force is looking for you."

"Do you really believe that I killed him, Thanh, after the work we have done together?"

"In this war I can believe anything."

Bolan motioned to the corpses turning in the eddy.

"Do you know any of them?"

The Vietnamese walked over and watched them go around.

"The Vietnamese I don't know. I think he is a tribesman. Meo, or Laotian."

"And the others?"

"We have seen them before. They are the foreigners." Thanh looked back at Bolan, his sunglasses reflecting the river and the sampans. It was a long look. Someone was going to have to kill Thanh very soon.

Bolan was pushing the bodies out into the current, when he heard Thanh's voice come from the bridge above.

"You want a reason, Sergeant? History repeats itself. The Council of Kings."

BOLAN LOOKED AT THE ROOM through the slatted vent of the locker. The coroners worked at an enamel table in the center of the white-tiled room. He breathed slowly, calmly, so that he remained perfectly still and could not be heard. The place was cool, even in his hiding place. Indeed, it was chilling.

They unzipped the bag and turned their heads away as the odor escaped. Bolan saw a young man's face. The kid was maybe eighteen or nineteen years old, the tendons tightened into a grimace. They pulled the bag off him and began stripping away his tattered fatigues.

"Jesus Christ," said one of the coroners. "Here I

was looking for a bullet wound and he doesn't have any."

"Bled to death," said Morgan.

They stripped him naked and dead.

"I've seen this before," Morgan told the other coroner. "Every time they do one of these pacification programs we get the weirdest sights. This guy was reckoning on slipping it to a slope, okay? But she's the enemy. She gets a tube, or a toilet roll or whatever, and lines it with razor blades. Bob from Nebraska here gives her one in the hut and bang. The way blood pumps into erectile tissue, I'd say he was dead in fifteen seconds."

The other man was slitting the body open down the belly and letting the guts drop through the well in the table into a sealed bin below. Bolan heard the slick plop as the intestinal matter hit bottom.

"What are they going to tell this kid's mother?"

"Maybe they'll give him the Purple Heart."

They worked, cleaning the cavity and stuffing it with the cotton and formaldehyde. The man across from Morgan broke the silence.

"Shouldn't we lay low for a while?" he said softly.

"No problem," Morgan replied. "They're going to put that crazy young sergeant in the slammer for good."

The odor from the corpse drifted over to Bolan. It invaded the locker, filling his nostrils with the stench of putrefaction.

The coroner brought over a cardboard box and began placing bags of white powder among the cotton in the GI's gut space. Dr. Morgan walked over to his desk and unlocked a drawer. He took out some papers and a pencil.

"What's the serial number on this one?"

The other man read the number and Morgan copied it down.

"What does Putnam say about all this?" asked Morgan's partner.

"Don't mention his name again. Especially to any of the others. We're all better off if Putnam's name is kept out of it."

"I see he's really keeping his nose clean."

"You could say that. You going to sew that one up?"

"Soon as I finish packing him. Jesus, this guy has enough dope in him to supply New York for a month."

Morgan finished writing and put the papers back in the drawer and locked it. Then he took off his coat and walked toward the locker. Bolan watched as his face grew nearer.

"That's not my concern, Mike, my boy," said Morgan, his voice suddenly very near, filling the locker. "Not my concern."

Bolan's adrenaline started its pounding effect. The gun felt good in his hands. Morgan pulled open the locker door and then dropped his coat in horror. The big bastard stepped from the locker, unwrapping his big frame even as he pressed the Colt M16A1 into Morgan's genital area. Morgan stopped breathing. He stared up into a pair of crazy blue eyes.

Mike was stitching, unaware of Bolan's presence.

"You got a lot of balls, running an operation like

this, Morgan," Mike said. He pulled a long stitch through the kid's corpse.

Bolan cut the air with the voice of the guillotine. "Not much longer he hasn't. Drop the knife and get against the wall."

Mike turned, still holding the thread. Seeing Bolan, he obeyed. Morgan was wide-eyed, sweating and trembling. He tried to edge his genitals away from the gun barrel, but Bolan kept it jammed tight.

"Who is Putnam?"

Neither spoke.

Bolan pulled the hammer back with a resounding click.

"Tell me who Putnam is."

Morgan's voice shook. "Putnam is a guy, just a guy who tells me what to do. I don't know who he is."

"You lie to me again and I fire this thing."

Morgan stole a glance at Mike, then looked back at the big bastard holding the gun. His lips trembled.

A knock on the door. Bolan told Morgan to answer.

"It's me, Jones," said a voice through the door. "You finished yet?"

The door swung open. A guard walked in, rifle slung over his shoulder. He saw Bolan and cocked it, bringing it up to fire.

"Don't!" yelled Morgan.

Bolan pushed Morgan away and swung the Colt up to the guard. Bolan waited for a split second to see if the guard would fire.

The guard brought the gun up until it pointed at Bolan's face.

Bolan blew away the guard's face.

Mike whimpered in fear. He shook.

Bolan kicked each man in the head, swiftly and surely. He pulled the keys from Morgan's pocket, as the man slumped and groaned. A whistle blew shrilly somewhere in the building.

Bolan tore open the drawer and stuffed the papers into his shirt. Blood from the guard's head flowed between his boots in a crimson rivulet. Then came the sound of rushing feet.

Bolan slid out the workroom door. Two guards rounded the corner, SMGs at the ready. They pulled up to fire. Bolan sent the first spinning back with a roaring blast from the Colt. The second gunner tore the wall open with slugs. Bolan closed his eyes against the spray of hot plaster and crouched, then fired at the muzzle-flash. The room fell silent.

Sirens screamed across the tarmac. A troop carrier pulled up, guards spilling from the back. Bolan sprang, making for the other door.

In the bright heat outside, Bolan put on his mirror sunglasses and holstered his gun. The truck was idling, its driver ready.

Bolan walked up and shrugged. "I can't find that asshole anywhere," he said.

The driver looked down at him. "What the hell is going on, anyway?"

"I don't know," Bolan said, opening the door of the truck and yanking the driver out. The driver sprawled on the tarmac as Bolan shifted into gear and roared off.

THERE WAS A SOFT CRACK of billiard balls. Carpet spread beneath his feet. There were women here.

Colonel Harlan Winters, known as "Howlin' Harlan" in the officer corps, looked up from his whiskey at the officers' club and nearly choked.

"Bolan," he managed to get out, "how the hell did you get in here?" Winters looked furtively around the room.

Bolan turned his back to the rest of the room and stood at ease beside Winters. From inside his shirt he withdrew a sheaf of papers. He lay them on the polished wood of the bar in front of Winters.

"You shouldn't have risked coming here."

"I'm safer here," replied Bolan.

"Jesus Christ," muttered Winters as he scanned the papers. "You were the one who blew open this heroin thing?"

"They accused me of killing Jim Naiman in order to shut me up," Bolan said.

Winters read on compulsively. Bolan stole a glance behind at the officers' club. They might have been in Nevada someplace, from the looks of it—carpeting, lamps, pool table. In the next room a movie was showing. Sentimental music sounded through the wall. Bolan listened to the dialogue. A woman was trying to dissuade her soldier from going to war.

Bolan ordered a drink. Who was the actor? Henry Fonda? No, Ronald Reagan. The voices were distorted as they came through the wall.

"You're a special man, Bill. You have courage. More than I do, I guess. Please stay."

"I'm not so special. I just fight for what I believe. As long as there's a bully to fight, I'll be there...."

The music swelled; they were probably kissing on an airstrip or a ship.

Winters whistled and looked up. Bolan caught the faint breath of whiskey.

"This is a dirty business, isn't it?"

"As dirty as it gets."

"Look, my advice is don't get too hot about it. I've been hearing rumors about the CIA transporting raw heroin for the Laotians in return for raids on VC camps inside the Laotian border. Maybe we need that."

"We don't need what we're getting now. The VC in the Mekong get anything they want—weapons, supplies, anything. The so-called intelligence we've been going on is useless. Our boys are getting slaughtered. Buddy knew it on that mission."

Winters took a thoughtful sip of his drink.

"You're right about the intelligence. I could do better with a Ouija board. But we can't let the VC keep Laos as their supply depot. Anyway, it's too late now. The whole thing is under official investigation."

"Who's doing the investigating?"

"The CIA. Top level, here in Saigon. Putnam himself is heading the investigation."

"Putnam?"

"What's the matter?" Winters had seen Bolan's face freeze.

Bolan felt a sense of desolation sweep through him, of justice torn and shredded, scattered to the winds.

"Putnam is the one running the operation."

Winters threw up his arms.

"Listen, Colonel," Bolan said urgently. "You have to stash those papers away until I find a way to get around Putnam. I'm dropping out of sight. I'm going back to the Mekong."

Winters leaned forward and looked piercingly at Bolan. "Don't go back to the Mekong now, Mack. Anywhere but there. We're getting casualties way beyond anyone's predictions. It's a mess, a blood-bath."

Through the wall came heroic music. Must be near the end of the movie, Bolan thought.

Winters continued uneasily. "You've been too much at the front line, Mack. You're starting to get that look in your eye."

"You know how it is as well as I do," said Bolan. "There is no front line. The front line is every-where."

Winters stopped Bolan before he walked through the door. "Mack, be careful you don't go over the edge. Nam does that to people."

Bolan knew now, standing in that officers' bar, just how Buddy felt when he was shaving his head. "I'm already over the edge," he said.

MOSQUITO NETTING hung diaphanous in the moon-light. Bolan felt the fatigue working on his mind as he stood over the bed. He must be careful now. For a moment Buddy appeared in hallucination, squatting on the floor with his knife at Bolan's feet.

Bolan pulled back the netting. Vu Quoc Thanh lay

sleeping. The moon illumined him with a corpselike pallor.

Bolan sat on the edge of the bed. Thanh shot upright, feeling for his gun. Bolan grabbed him by the wrist until he gained his senses. Thanh wiped the sweat from his neck and torso, finally his face.

"What is the Council of Kings?" whispered Bolan.

Thanh faced him, the moon behind him glowing on his shoulders. His face was in darkness.

"The Council of Kings is the name given to those who run your war."

"The Pentagon?"

"No. Intelligence. The people who sell the war to the generals and the money-makers. The people who give your country a reason to send its youth to their deaths."

"What do they have to do with the heroin?"

Thanh waved the question away with a bony white hand.

"The heroin is a minor thing, useful to the Council for making deals, making money. But you and your people are being lied to. Many times I tried to warn the American intelligence people that the VC were strong—stronger than they could imagine. But they would not listen."

"Why not?"

"They wanted to tell their people that they could win the war. Now they are finding out that I was right, but they cannot admit it. For years I told them, but they ignored me."

"We can win it. If we can only cut off the VC supply routes—"

"You don't understand. This country has been invaded and occupied by foreign armies for thousands of years. The people here have always driven them out, sooner or later. Don't you understand? The only way to win this war is to kill every man, woman and child."

Bolan did not know what to say. He looked mutely at the figure crouching beside him.

"You have already started to do that," continued Thanh. "Look at what you do in the villages. Are you making friends there? You give the Vietcong more supporters everywhere your army goes."

"But the camps—we get more and more people in our camps—"

"Simply because the people must avoid the American bombs. You cannot promise these people anything that the French have not already promised. Look where it got the French. We will always win."

Bolan sat rooted to the bed. There was a heaviness in his limbs he had never felt before. He had suckered Thanh with his talk, and the guy had fallen for it.

"Did you say 'we'?" asked Bolan.

"No," said Thanh, reaching for a cigarette. "I didn't."

Bolan sprang. With one big hand he smothered Thanh's face, pressing down into the bed. He rose over Thanh and sank his knee into the smaller man's gut.

"You joined them, didn't you, Thanh? It was you who got to Buddy first."

Thanh looked up at the big bastard who held his life in his hands. Bolan saw that his eyes held fear, but no more than fear. He could see that Thanh had expected it to end this way. Had expected it since childhood.

Bolan gently took out his knife and cut into Thanh's throat, holding him until the body stopped jerking.

Then he ransacked the room feverishly. In his pocket Buddy's ear began to twitch. Bolan ignored it. He knew it was fatigue and not reality, but all the same he felt the ear jump as if it were alive. Thanh's bowels had let go, and the room had begun to smell of the foulness of death.

Nothing escaped Bolan's hand. He knew the thing was somewhere in the room, though he could not say how he knew. From the bookshelf he withdrew a worn copy of *Les Misérables*. Holding it by the spine, he let the contents fall from between the leaves.

It lay there on the desk, downy and tattered like a piece of litter. Buddy's map.

BOLAN SAT in a padded chair, looking at a picture on Putnam's desk of the man's family at Disneyland. They were stuffing their faces with cotton candy. Bolan closed his eyes against the image. Morning sun glared through the office blinds.

The door opened for a senior bureaucrat looking well groomed in a gray suit. Maybe he was taking someone to lunch. He crossed the room and thrust his hand toward Bolan, the essence of ease and authority.

"Dick Putnam. You're Johnson?"

"That's right," said Bolan. "Phil Johnson."

"You know something about this heroin thing?" asked Putnam, settling himself into his chair behind the fortress of a desk.

"Yeah," said Bolan. "I know a lot about it. I know you run the operation. You use the dead bodies of American soldiers to ship your heroin. I know you lie about the strength of the Vietcong. I know you get a lot of innocent kids killed or maimed for life."

Bolan was surprised at his own sureness. He was a young man unused to going too far.

Putnam's face had become a mask of hate and panic. He sat immobilized.

Bolan continued to drive words home like a jackhammer. "You scar people. You use them for your own purposes and then kill them. You killed Naiman and blamed me for it. You use your position of trust as if it were your whore."

Putnam's eyes darted to the photo of his family. Bolan drove on mercilessly. "You could say I know something about it. I lost a buddy because of you."

Furious, Putnam reached across the desk and grabbed the picture frame as a weapon. Bolan smashed his fist down on Putnam's, breaking the hand and shattering the glass and the frame that it held. Putnam cried out, his face white and twisted with pain, and he put his injured hand between his thighs.

Bolan reached around Putnam's throat and pulled him across the desk with a powerful jerk of his shoulder. Putnam lay wheezing, his head on the desk, the corners of his mouth wet with spittle.

"It's not me you want," the CIA man gasped. "I answer to others. Please..."

"I'll bet you answer to others," Bolan said. He spread his fingers around Putnam's neck and jaw and applied pressure. "What others?"

"The Council," Putnam hissed against the constriction around his throat.

"Who on the Council?"

Putnam looked at his assailant in panic. Bolan pressed down hard.

"Civilians," the guy squealed. "They're not soldiers... nothing to do with the war. Except Heiss— Karl Heiss..."

"And the civilians?"

"Gunrunners... just gunrunners and money-men. They buy the heroin...."

"Names." Bolan introduced more significant pressure.

"Marcello. Andriola. Canzonari. That's it...."

This rat was living up to its name.

Bolan pulled the remains of the map from his pocket. Putnam clamped his jaws shut. Bolan loosened them with a punch to the temple, then pulled them apart until Putnam's fillings gleamed in the sun.

"This is for Buddy," he said. "Don't you ever forget." Bolan pushed the map into Putnam's mouth and rammed it down his throat until Putnam gagged.

Bolan turned to leave. At the door he looked back. Putnam rolled off the desk, his right hand hanging useless and discolored. The CIA man began to began to vomit, retching painfully.

"Chew that over with your Council of Kings," Bolan said. He slammed the door and marched down the corridor, moving purposefully out of there.

Bolan knew a little more about himself now, a lot more about brotherhood and loss. And he knew for absolute sure that he would survive to shove injustice down the throats of many more vermin to come. He had heard the names—and had just heard the call.

And he was still so damn near over the edge.

So he prayed for his family, because he was scared, and he vowed that he would never voluntarily share this dreadful war with his kin, his mother and father, his sister, Cindy, and younger brother Johnny, all back home.

And then Bolan prayed that in his personal war to come, the inevitable war seeded in this corruption called Vietnam, the enemy would be *his* and *his alone*.

No buddies.

And now, back to war. Back to Mohawk time in the Mekong. . . .

MORE ADVENTURE NEXT MONTH WITH

MACK BOLAN

#80 Running Hot

School for slaughter

A new wave of crime is rocking France. Each incident is made to look like the work of foreign terrorists—but the atrocities are in fact part of a vastly more ambitious plan.

Deep in a desolate region of the country is a place where young dropouts and derelicts are educated in the art of terrorism. The Executioner knows very well the perverse principles of this "institute of higher learning" and aims to close the death school forever.

If it's the last thing he ever does.

GOLD
EAGLE

Available wherever paperbacks are sold.

A new tradition in publishing
SUPERBOLANS!

Gold Eagle's SuperBolan books are making history. Twice as long as the regular series books, the SuperBolan adventures pack more punch, deliver more out-and-out action than any other books of their kind on the market!

STONY MAN DOCTRINE

stands as a beacon of hope for all readers bugged by the rise of international terrorism.

"A blockbuster!"
— *New York Daily News*

TERMINAL VELOCITY

broke new ground for Gold Eagle readers by taking Mack Bolan on a high-adventure trip around the world.

"It's a Bolan hit!"
— *Daily Mercury*

responded directly to readers' needs for a deeper, more personal view of Bolan's life by teaming up the big guy with his long-lost brother, Johnny. The book hits home with deadly impact. No wonder the *New York Times* calls these Bolan adventures "today's hottest books for men!"

AND NOW...